"No, I'm not nuts," she said slowly. "You're not a little girl anymore, honey, and if that's the way it's done in Hollywood . . ."

I covered my ears with my hands. I didn't want to hear any of it.

"So maybe you should consider . . ."

"No!" I shouted. "There's no way I'm going to screw some old fart of a producer just on the chance that he *may* give me some dinky little part in his stupid ol' movie."

"Honey, I didn't say you should; I just said that maybe you should consider it, think about it," my mother said tactfully.

"No way!" I yelled, then grabbed my purse and ran out of the apartment.

I got onto Sunset Boulevard and began to walk. I needed to walk, to burn off some of my energy, my boredom and frustration. And I needed to think. What the hell was I doing in Hollywood? Where was my life going? No place, it seemed.

I walked along, it must have been for a good three miles, and I soon found myself in the Sunset Strip area. I wasn't dressed up, just wearing jeans and a plain blouse, but I couldn't walk a block without guys calling out to me from passing cars.

"Hey, pretty lady, want a ride?" was one of the more polite invitations. What some of them said, I wouldn't even repeat. There were so many different approaches these guys used to "introduce themselves" to a girl, and all the approaches led to the same place, as far as I could see — bed. Right then, I wasn't the least bit interested in any of them. In fact, I was so used to being approached that a lot of the time I didn't even take any notice.

FADE TO BLACK

HOLLOWAY HOUSE PUBLISHING COMPANY
LOS ANGELES, CALIFORNIA

PUBLISHED BY
Holloway House Publishing Company
8060 Melrose Avenue
Los Angeles, California 90046

All rights reserved. No part of this book may be reproduced or transmitted in any form or by any means, electronic or mechanical, including photocopying, recording or by any information storage and retrieval system, without permission in writing from the Publisher. Copyright © 1981 by Leo Guild. Any similarity to persons living or dead is purely coincidental.

International Standard Book Number 0-87067-015-8
Printed in the United States of America

CHAPTER 1

I grew up in Hollywood. That is, I came of age in Hollywood not too long after my mother, full of ambition, brought me here to Tinseltown on a Greyhound bus. I was just barely fourteen, but she believed with all her heart and soul that I would soon become a star.

It was back in early 1968, but I can remember the day we arrived as though it were yesterday. The big, shiny bus pulled away from the traffic on the crowded, smog-enshrouded Hollywood Freeway and soon we were riding through the streets of Hollywood. I was in awe as I looked out the tinted window at the palm trees; new hi-rise office buildings next to old-fashioned ones; small, neat apartment houses and private homes. The structures were different than they were back in Saginaw, Michigan, and I noticed it right away. Here the houses all looked like they were made of gingerbread and many of them were oddly shaped, jutting out in all directions. Once in a while, I saw a straight-lined brick building, but not often. There were small stores and movie houses and everything was so colorful. Most of all, I liked the tall, graceful palm trees on every block.

I watched the people on the street, hoping to see a movie star so I could point him or her out to my mother.

But I didn't see anyone I recognized. Little did I know that by 1968 there were no more movie stars in Hollywood; by then they had all moved to much nicer areas, such as Beverly Hills, Bel Air and Malibu out at the beach. A couple of times, I noticed young women walking along in flashy hot-pants suits, glamorously made up, swinging their bodies along confidently. I wondered if they were actresses; they were probably hookers.

I looked over at Mama. She was leaning her head back on the headrest of the high-back seat, her face more relaxed than I had ever seen it, an expression of euphoria on her face. She had always wanted to come to Hollywood, and it had taken almost all the money she had managed to save to get us here on the bus, which, to me, had been a luxury trip.

Mama noticed me looking at her and smiled. "Isn't it wonderful, baby? We're finally here."

I nodded and looked out the window again. I wondered if we were going to live here in Hollywood. I hadn't noticed all that many black people walking along. Some, but most of the people were white.

"When I was a young girl," Mama was saying, "I was pretty, too, real pretty. But you, Mary Clarissa, you're just gorgeous. And you have a beautiful figure, also. That's mighty important out here." She laughed to herself. "It's very important anywhere, matter of fact."

I winced, hunching up in my seat so that my large, well-shaped breasts seemed to almost disappear. In school, the tough, rowdy boys were always grabbing at me for a feel and calling out obscenities. If anything, my sexy, well-developed body was an embarrassment to me, so much so that I very rarely went to school, even though I found the work interesting and enjoyable, especially Social Studies, a combination of geography and history. I was always interested in people. But it was hard to learn anything in the school I went to, where there were gangs and fights and almost all the boys carried knives. Some of the girls did, too, and many of the boys even had guns. I never fit in that environment, so I didn't have too many friends. In the slums of Saginaw, I was a misfit. But that was all over now, I hoped. Mama said that here in Hollywood a good figure was a tremendous asset to a girl, and I believed her, sort of.

Lately it was hard for me to believe anything completely. The previous summer there had been terrible, frightening riots throughout Michigan, beginning in Detroit and filtering down through Flint and Saginaw. There was burning and looting, and I was beaten up and raped in a filthy, rat-infested alley one block from our tenement. My physical wounds healed quickly; I was a healthy young girl. But psychologically it was a different story. I was in shock for a period of months.

Mama cried and cried. "My poor baby, she ain't ever going to come out of it." That's when she decided we were going to relocate to Hollywood, and I think it gave me hope, because I soon got better.

"Nothing like that will happen to me in Hollywood, will it Mama?" I asked anxiously.

"No, baby, nothing like that will happen to you ever again," Mama had reassured me. "Certainly not in Hollywood. Here in Michigan, everything's always been lousy . . ." For her, it always had been so; the riots that summer were simply the last straw.

As the bus pulled into the small terminal on Vine Street, I drifted back into the present.

"Hollywood!" the driver intoned, and it was music to my ears.

We got off the bus, carrying our two small, worn-out suitcases. Not that we traveled much; the suitcases were worn out because Mama had purchased them at a thrift store, used, for fifty cents each.

"Great deal!" she had proclaimed proudly. Any money saved in Saginaw brought our big trip closer. Getting to Hollywood was our only hope, she felt, and I did too.

The bus pulled away and we stood there on Vine Street, taking it all in. People walked up and down the street in summer clothing, just about. They seemed to be strolling, in no particular hurry.

Mama laughed; it was good to see her happy. "Back in Michigan," she said, "we'd be freezing right now." She was right. Our dingy little roach-infested flat was supposed to be heated, but most of the time the radiator didn't work.

I thought of my father. He probably wasn't freezing; by now he'd have read Mama's note and he'd be stoned drunk. Mama didn't tell him where we were going, but it wouldn't take him long to figure out that we'd be heading for New York or Hollywood. He'd then go down to the bar-and-grill on the corner of our teeming, congested block, drink himself sick, bragging to his pals about how he was going to "track down that no-good, lazy woman," and then he'd go home and sleep it off. At least, that's how I imagined he'd react. I wondered if my father would miss me. When I was a small child he had been a good father and husband. He had gone to work every day at a factory in nearby Midland, Michigan, and on Saturdays he'd take Mama and me on an outing to the country or to a movie in town. Sometimes we'd even ride all the way to Detroit, which I loved. And on Sundays, Mama and I would go to church — my father would sleep late — then go home, have lunch and all three of us would go out visiting friends or relatives. But the accident changed all that. One day, my father caught his hand in some machinery at the plant. That day, I remember, he came home with his hand all bandaged up.

"The doctor says it probably will never heal up," he announced, as Mama cried quietly. "Hey, woman, stop that crying!" he yelled. "It means I don't have to work anymore. I'll be getting disability pay."

But Mama kept right on crying. She was smart enough to know that with too much time on his hands and no work to do, a man soon becomes bored and unhappy. She was right. Papa soon found a hobby, in fact, two hobbies: drinking and women. Mama got a job as a waitress and most of the time I was alone.

One day I came home from school and heard some odd noises in the house. The bedroom door was shut tight. When I opened it, I gasped. There was my father lying in the bed, stark naked, all entwined with a woman I'd never seen before. She was nude, too, and the whole thing scared the hell out of me. I closed the door, backed away and hid in the dark hallway closet for what seemed like an eternity. When my mother came home from work, there was a terrible fight, which ended with my father slamming out of the apartment and my mother holding a cold compress over a bruised, bleeding eye.

When I finally came out of the closet, she hugged me, sobbing. "Someday, Mary Clarissa, we'll get out of here. I promise you that, baby," she went on, "it won't be like this forever . . ."

"What were Papa and that lady doing in there?" I asked her. I was only about seven at the time.

Mama didn't answer.

"Was it something terrible?" I knew they weren't fighting.

"No, Mary Clarissa," Mama finally answered. "It wasn't anything terrible in itself, but . . ." I guess she didn't want to scare me into having sex problems in the future.

"Then why did you get so mad at Papa that he hurt you

and ran out of the house?" The whole thing made no sense to me.

Still holding the cold, wet washcloth over her swollen eye, she looked at me as though trying to think of something to say. She couldn't.

"Never mind, baby," she said softly, but I could tell she was very uncomfortable. "When you're a big girl, you'll understand."

I stamped my foot and pouted. "Mama, that's what you always say! I am a big girl, right now!"

She didn't answer me, but got up and, still holding the cold compress over her eye, began to fix us something to eat.

"Fried potatoes and some nice scrambled eggs with onions," she said in a monotone, "that'll cheer you up, honey." But she was the one who needed cheering up.

Now, standing in front of the bus terminal, I switched my mind off the unpleasant memories.

"So what do we do now?" I asked Mama.

"Well," she replied, "let's get us something to eat." Food was still Mama's solution, which was probably why she was quite hefty.

We went through the glass doors into the small, dingy Hollywood bus terminal, where I noticed a seedy-looking woman stretched out on one of the wooden benches, asleep and snoring loudly. As we walked by, I saw that two of her front teeth were missing, and she smelled ghastly.

Mama put the two old suitcases down on a bench. "Here, Mary Clarissa, you stay and watch these suitcases so that no one steals them."

She walked over to the back of the little terminal and fished around in her purse for change. There were coffee and soda machines, and a machine that dispensed candy bars and cheese and cracker snacks. I never was one for junk food, but I hadn't eaten in a long time and I was very hungry. I wished she would hurry up.

I was beginning to feel uncomfortable standing there alone; I seemed to sense someone watching me. I was right. I looked up and saw a big, tough-looking black dude approaching, a gleam in his eyes.

He ambled up close to me, and I tensed up. "Hey, sexy mama, what's happening, babe?" he said in a low voice.

I looked toward where Mama was standing, fumbling with the change, pulling on the handles of the candy machine. I wanted to rush over to her, but the man was standing between me and the two suitcases, and I couldn't risk losing all our things. I didn't know what to do and I was beginning to panic.

"Just buzz into town, lovely lady?" the guy was saying.

Without looking back at him, I nodded. I should have called out to my mother, but I was too scared to think.

"Say, you are sexy," he went on, putting his hand around my narrow waist.

I cringed.

He laughed. "What are you so scared of? Come on, let's you and me go out and have some fun . . ."

Now Mama was coming back, loaded down with paper cups of coffee and packaged food from the machines. She walked right up to us, set the coffee and food down on the bench, and stared right into the man's eyes.

"Anything I can help you with, young man?" she asked in a stern, school teacher voice. "This is my daughter . . ."

The man's manner changed instantly, and he took his hand off me. "Well, uh, no, ma'am," he stammered, while Mama kept staring at him. "I was just saying, welcome to town . . ." With that, he turned and sauntered out of the bus terminal.

I was standing there, shaking.

My mother looked at me. "Mary Clarissa," she said

softly, "of course you do have to be careful, but you've also got to realize that not every man is a rapist."

The word "rape" was enough to make my stomach churn, and Mama saw that.

"I'm sorry, honey," she said. "I just want you to learn how to handle yourself. I know you're only fourteen years old, but you've got the body of a woman and you appear to be much more mature than you are . . ."

All this conversation in the middle of a bus terminal? I looked around self-consciously, but no one was paying any attention to us. The woman derelict kept right on snoring, and the man behind the counter selling tickets seemed to be oblivious to everything but whomever he happened to be waiting on.

Mama noticed that I was looking all around. "You've got to have more confidence in yourself," she said. "You've got to stop worrying about everybody and what they think." She smiled. "After all, I believe you're going to be a big star, you know that."

I couldn't really imagine it, but it sounded good, like an escape from reality. My face must have brightened up, because my mother looked happy.

"Now, honey, let's sit down here and have our lunch."

We sat there for nearly half an hour, eating candy and cheese and cracker snacks and drinking weak coffee with sugar and watered-down cream in it, out of paper cups which quickly became soggy. Another bus pulled in, and we watched as people, all different types, disembarked. There was a mother traveling with four small children; her suitcase popped open and all her belongings fell out all over the dirty terminal floor. Mama and I helped them pick everything up and stuff it back into the old suitcase, which was in even worse condition than our two used ones.

"Everyone coming off the bus looks so poor," I whispered to Mama.

"I guess rich folks don't take the bus," she observed. "Rich folks fly to where they're going."

Four hippies with long, straggly hair wandered in from the street and proceeded to panhandle. They fanned out around the terminal, asking anyone and everyone for money, except for the woman derelict, who was still sleeping but had ceased snoring.

"Hey, man, got any loose change?" one of the hippies asked my mother.

Mama stood up and faced the bedraggled young man. "No, I certainly don't," she said quietly and with dignity. "Now why don't you go get yourself cleaned up and go out and look for a job?"

The hippie boy was taken aback; usually people either gave him change or merely ignored him.

I looked away, embarrassed at my mother's outspokenness, although I agreed with what she told the boy.

"Say, what are you, some kind of a teacher?" the hippie said sarcastically, but with a tinge of respect.

"No," Mama replied. "I work as a waitress because I didn't get myself an education."

The boy smiled. "Well, I don't blame you. I was in college for two years, but I dropped out. College is not where it's at . . ."

"It's not?" said my mother sternly. "Then where is it at? Panhandling, begging in the streets? I don't know what you kids are rebelling against. The world's far from perfect, but there's still plenty you can do." I suppose Mama was afraid that I might go that route; a lot of kids did back in the sixties. But dropping out and being a hippie was the farthest thing from my mind.

Soon, the other three hippies joined the boy and they made their way to the door. The boy turned and waved at Mama.

"Hey, man," he called out, waving, "take care of yourself!" He made the peace sign with his hand.

"Who's the old broad?" one of the hippie girls asked, in a voice loud enough for us to hear.

"No one," the boy answered, "and someone. And everyone!"

They all turned and made the peace sign at us, and Mama had to shake her head and smile.

We sat down and finished the rest of our junk food lunch. So far, it was nothing like I'd read in the movie magazines, but we had, in fact, arrived in Hollywood.

CHAPTER 2

"Mama, it doesn't look like too many black people live around here," I said. "Maybe they don't rent to black people in Hollywood. Maybe we should go to another neighborhood."

"Pshaw," was my mother's reply. "There's mostly show business people here. And people in show business are 'color blind,' you know."

So far, I hadn't seen anyone who looked like he or she was in show business since we got off the bus. In the two and a half hours since our arrival in movieland, we had been walking up and down the side streets, in and out of small apartment buildings, looking for an apartment to rent.

One building we stopped at had a huge, green weather-beaten sign outside proclaiming, "Luxury apartments, all-electric kitchens, swimming pool, sun deck. Adults only, no pets."

"From now on, by the way," my mother told me, "you just say you're eighteen. You can pass for it, and it'll make things a lot easier for us."

I smiled. "You mean, I don't have to go to school?" I asked, delighted.

"We'll talk about it later," Mama replied. I guess she felt that future movie and television stars didn't need that much of an education. I knew she always regretted her own lack of schooling, but I guess that was different; the old adage about parents wanting for their kids everything they themselves lacked didn't apply to my Mama.

My mother rang the manager's doorbell and a plump woman in a housecoat and hair rollers opened the door.

"Yeah, what is it?" the woman asked, looking us up and down.

My mother explained that we had just arrived in Hollywood and that we were looking for an apartment.

"Sorry, no vacancies," the manager snapped, slamming the door.

We received similar receptions at various buildings we tried.

"Well," Mama said, "we don't know that it's because we're black. Maybe it's because we're standing here with our two old suitcases. They might be afraid that we're transients with no jobs, and that we won't have the rent money."

I nodded, but I was dubious.

"I've got an idea," my mother said. "The next building we go to, we'll put the suitcases off to the side so they can't see them. And I won't say anything about just arriving here."

"I hope it works," I said.

"So do I," my mother shook her head from side to side. "Otherwise, we'll have to check in at a motel, and that's a waste of money, even a cheap one. I've got almost two hundred and fifty dollars in cash left; I think we can get a decent apartment with that, and even have a couple of dollars left over until I can find a job." Remember, it was 1968, and rents were still cheap in Hollywood.

It was late afternoon and still light out when we came upon a small park.

"Isn't it pretty?" I said.

Mama agreed, and we walked into the park and sat down on a bench to rest for a while. In the park there was a huge bronze statue of a naked man, with a plaque explaining that it was a tribute to the famous movie idol of the 1920s, Rudolph Valentino.

People were walking and running their dogs, and children were playing — white, black and Mexican.

"See?" Mama pointed out. "I told you, this is a mixed neighborhood, not only whites. We'll get an apartment today, you'll see."

Across the street from the park, we noticed a rather sprawled out, two-story building, with a sign, "Vacancies," large enough for us to read from across the street.

We went over and, as my mother suggested, hid the two suitcases behind a bush. Mama rang the manager's doorbell. Soon, a curtain moved on the window next to the door.

"Hey, Dad!" we heard a child's voice inside. "There's some coloreds out there ringing the bell!"

I was ready to leave, but my mother held her ground. We could hear the sound of a saxophone; whoever was playing it was in dire need of lessons.

The door opened wide and a fat white man stood there, no shirt on, cigarette hanging from his lips. "Yeah?" he asked. "Whadda ya want?"

"I'm Mrs. Hattie Stevens," my mother said with her usual dignity, "and this is my daughter, Mary Clarissa . . ."

"Shut up in there!" the fat man interrupted, calling into the apartment. "I told you not to fool with that thing until you learn how! You can't play worth a damn anyway!"

The raucous sound of the saxophone stopped abruptly.

The manager turned back to us and smiled through a puff of cigarette smoke. "My wife, Mae. Good woman but she don't have an ear for music at all. I'm the musician in the family, but I don't get enough work."

Mama returned the smile while I just stared at the guy. "As I was saying," my mother continued, "we're looking for an apartment. We chose your building because of the nice park across the street. Hollywood is getting so congested lately, it's nice to be near grass and trees."

My eyes opened wide. Compared to what we were used to, Hollywood was like the country, park or no park.

"Well, thank you," the manager said. "Glad you like the building."

"Do you have an apartment you can show us?" Mama asked. "If there's nothing available, we can come back. We're not in any hurry." Maybe *she* should have been the actress!

"No, no, no," the manager held his hand up. "As a matter of fact, I have two apartments I can show you. You can have your choice."

"Wonderful," replied my mother.

"Just wait here a minute while I get my keys," the fat man said. "I'd ask you to come in, but the apartment's a mess." He turned his head and called inside, "My wife's too busy to keep the place clean!"

In a moment, he returned with a huge set of keys, and began to lead the way. I didn't know what to do; I didn't want to leave the suitcases, but I was afraid to kill the deal by pulling them out.

The decision was made for me. "Those your suitcases?" the manager asked, seeing them. "Better take them with you; they might get stolen around here. Damn people'd steal the you-know-what out of the toilet if they thought they could get away with it." He stopped himself. "No one in this building would, of course. But some of the other managers around here will rent to anybody. What I'm gonna do is get up a petition against them . . ." The man went on and on.

We rented a shabbily furnished one-room apartment with a small kitchen for $88.50 a month. My mother paid the man first and last month's rent, in cash, leaving us more spending money than we thought we'd have.

"I'm supposed to take a $25 cleaning fee, non-refundable, but I'll tell you what. If you want to clean it up yourself, I'll waive the fee." He winked. "Besides, it's my wife who does the cleaning, so it's really a rip-off. She can't clean any better than she can play the sax." He laughed uproariously as he handed my mother the house keys and mail box keys.

We went back to his apartment and waited outside while he wrote up a receipt for the cash.

"I'm also supposed to get a buck-fifty key deposit," he informed us, "but you don't look like folks who would lose keys, so I'll skip that too."

"Thank you very much, sir," said Mama.

"Oh, by the way, my name's Stanley." He winked again. "But everybody calls me Stan!" Apparently he thought this was hilarious too; he burst out laughing.

Mama smiled politely while again, I just stared at him. He was quite a character.

The man looked back at me, and I could tell he found me very attractive. "You're a beautiful young lady. I'm sorry," he said, "what's your name again?"

"Mary Clarissa," I said quietly.

"Mary Clarissa," he repeated. "You have a lovely daughter, Hattie," he said to Mama. "How old are you, Mary Clarissa? About twenty?"

I gulped. "Eighteen," I stammered, although his guessing me to be twenty made it easier to lie and say that I was eighteen. If he had guessed my correct age, I probably couldn't have lied at all.

Mama, however, kept her cool throughout. "Well, thank you very much for everything, Stan," she said. "I guess we'll go get settled now."

"Right," the manager agreed. "See you later, alligator!" He went inside the apartment and closed the door.

While we were still within earshot, we heard him call out, "See, Mae? Coloreds are no different than anyone else. See, I know how to get along with them. They like me."

Mama and I smiled at each other and went to get things in order in our new home.

"We'll scrub up the place later," my mother instructed. "Now, we'd better go out and buy some groceries, and odds and ends we'll need."

We walked a couple of blocks to a small grocery store, but my mother decided that it might be best to look for a supermarket where we could get everything cheaper. Two more blocks away we found a large Safeway, where we saved a lot of money, just as Mama had expected.

When we got back to the apartment, our arms loaded down with bags of groceries, I scoured the refrigerator while Mama unpacked the goodies.

After the perishable items were put in the refrigerator, Mama said, "It's still early. Let's go look around the neighborhood."

In Southern California, twilight lasts about five minutes after the sun goes down, and then it gets dark. We had never seen anything like this, being from back East, and we enjoyed the phenomenon as we walked along the residential, lower middle class streets of Hollywood, 1968. Recently, I took a little nostalgia trip and visited the "old neighborhood." It's become pretty rundown, almost a slum, and I was disappointed. But it's still the first place I lived in Hollywood, and it will always have a special meaning to me.

Mama and I walked a little way to Sunset Boulevard — not the famous Sunset Strip, that's a few miles west of where we were. We came upon a large thrift shop where we waded through a bunch of junk and came up with a very pretty centerpiece made of imitation wood bark and silky-looking artificial flowers, on sale for fifty cents. We also bought some cheap cooking and eating utensils, plus inexpensive dishes, bowls, and cups and saucers.

We arrived back at out new apartment loaded down with packages. We were really having fun.

"See?" Mama said. "I told you we'd have a place to live by the end of the day. And a good deal it is, too. That manager's a nut, but so what? He's harmless, I'm sure."

I frowned, remembering the way he had looked at me. But then, I thought, most guys looked at me that way, and my mother said my looks were an asset. I hoped she was right.

My mother made hot chocolate for us to drink while we cleaned up and got the place in order. Soon I noticed a faraway look in her eyes.

"Homesick, Mama?" I smiled.

"I was just thinking about your father," she said. "He was once such a good man, and I suppose he misses us."

"Do you want to go back?" I asked, half seriously. I missed him; after all, he was my father.

Mama's face turned hard as stone, a very rare expression for her. "No," she said firmly. "We're here, and there's no turning back now."

I was scrubbing the kitchen floor and I began to scrub it even harder. I wished there were some way of turning back, even though I knew Mama was right.

CHAPTER 3

Within a couple of days, my mother got a waitress job at a drive-in restaurant a few blocks away from the apartment, and she was overjoyed.

"It's not a bad place," she beamed, "and I can save plenty on bus fare." Everyone says that you must have a car in Los Angeles, but for us it was out of the question; the buses and our feet would have to do, at least for a while.

"Congratulations, Mama," I said, happy for her not only because we needed the money her job would bring in, but because I knew that she really loved to work, even as a waitress. "What are your hours?" I asked.

"Four in the afternoon until midnight," she told me. "I could have taken a daytime shift, but I want to be here during the day. We've got to find some way of launching an acting career for you, you know."

I had no idea of how to begin anything like that, and I didn't think my mother did either. But if I knew her, she would soon find out.

"What we've got to do first, I guess," my mother continued, "is get you some acting training. After all, you'll be going on auditions, and you'll have to know how to handle yourself."

"Isn't that kind of expensive?" I asked.

"Well, I found out that just a few blocks away, at Sunset Boulevard and Highland Avenue, there's a public high school, Hollywood High."

I felt a sinking feeling in the pit of my stomach. I had hoped that I wouldn't have to go back to high school. "Oh," I said, disappointed.

Mama knew what I was thinking about, and she laughed. "At Hollywood High, they have evening classes for adults, and I think with a little fast talking, we can get you enrolled in their acting class, which meets from seven in the evening until around 10:30. Also, it will be good that you won't have to be alone at night when I'm at work, at least not the whole time I'm at work."

"And it's not expensive?" I asked.

"Only a few dollars to enroll. The money they take out of my salary every week for taxes pays for public education; we might as well take advantage of it, right?"

"Right," I agreed. Mama was always so practical; it was the way she thought. Yet, she never wanted something for nothing, never expected anything unless she was prepared to pay in some way or another. I guess it was also a realistic way to think; my experience in life has shown me that no matter what you get, you have to pay for it.

A few evenings later, I found myself at the acting workshop of Hollywood High. I was scared to death. Not only did I not know the first thing about acting, but I felt that all the other acting students were staring at me, looking me up and down, especially the males. Though I wore the most loose-fitting clothes I had, it was impossible not to draw attention to my well-rounded, sexy figure. And I could tell that several of the aspiring actresses were jealous of me, although some of them were quite good-looking themselves. I must admit that I was kind of pleased that the girls seemed envious of me, especially since they were so pretty. I guess even then I had a competitive streak, although I wasn't really aware of it.

I sat in the back of the room, trying unsuccessfully to remain unobtrusive, especially to the acting coach, a good-looking, well-built man no more than thirty years old. To me, at fourteen, thirty was ancient, but he sure was attractive, and when he looked at me, I wasn't frightened.

"Mary Clarissa," the acting coach said when the class settled down. He looked down at an index card. "Mary Clarissa Stevens." He smiled. "Why don't you stand up and tell us something about yourself?"

This was it; I was terrified. I had expected that I would be singled out because I was joining the workshop in the middle of the term; everyone already knew each other. But I didn't realize that my knees would be shaking so hard.

I stood up as everyone turned around in their chairs to look at me. I cleared my throat. "My name is Mary Clarissa Stevens," I began in a shaky voice.

"You'll have to speak up," the teacher said. "Project your voice! You're an actress, aren't you?"

Me, an actress? I thought he was making fun of me, and I became even more nervous.

"No," I replied, looking down at the floor. "At least not yet. That is, my mother wants me to be an actress." I could hear laughter from the other acting students, and I felt like running out of the room.

"Mary Clarissa," the acting coach said, his deep voice resonating throughout the classroom, "why don't you just relax? You're among friends, and we're all just nervous as you are. Actors are always nervous about performing," he went on. "Don't you know that even the great Helen Hayes throws up before a performance?"

This brought knowing smiles from the other students.

Myself, I couldn't care less about Helen Hayes. I just wanted to get the hell out of there and go home.

"In fact," the coach said, "let's break the ice right now. Come up here." I walked self-consciously to the front of the room.

Tom, the acting teacher, had two scripts in his hand. "Here," he handed me one, "I'll read with you. When you go on auditions, they'll ask you to read for the part, and you might as well get used to it."

Tom started reading, and then I read my lines from the script, though it was shaking so hard in my hands that I could hardly see the typewritten words.

"That's fine," the coach said, when we had gotten through the scene, "but you need practice."

My reading must have been perfectly awful, though I was so relieved that it was over I didn't even think about whether it was good, bad or indifferent.

As I walked back to my seat, I overheard one of the actors whisper, "Can't act worth a damn, but she's got a nice ass."

"Yeah," another replied, "nice tits, too."

"*Great* tits," replied the first.

I got through the rest of the evening in a fog. When the class was finally over, Tom asked me to stay for a few minutes after the others had gone.

"I need you to fill out some forms," he explained.

I was leery, but decided to do what he asked.

He gave me some printed material to complete, and as he handed me the papers, he said, "I don't know if you have any acting talent, Mary Clarissa, but you're a very sexy, beautiful girl, and that's what it takes in this town."

"That's what my mother says," I mumbled.

He sat down on top of his desk, with his strong, muscular legs spread apart. "You could be a star, I'll bet," he said. "A black sex symbol."

"Look," I replied, "I don't know if I want to be any big sex symbol."

"Are you crazy?" he laughed. "That's the greatest thing to be. You'll make plenty of money, and be able to screw any guy you want." He got up and walked over to where I was sitting. He stood very close, and I could feel myself becoming aroused — he was a very sexy man. I fought the feeling.

"I'm only fourteen-years-old," I blurted out, jumping up. "And last year I was raped — got that? Now you just stay away from me?" I held up the pen I had been writing with, pointing it at him as though it were a knife.

The poor guy looked shocked. He held his hands up. "Whoa," he said, "take it easy. I wasn't planning on raping you! I'm not that kind of a guy."

I relaxed a bit; he did seem sincere.

"You're going to have to get used to guys making passes at you," he went on. "You're a real knockout, you know."

I didn't answer him; I hadn't yet learned to be proud of my face and figure. So far, my looks had caused me nothing but trouble, first in the ghetto, and now here.

"You're not supposed to be in this class," Tom said, "since you're only fourteen. But I'll tell you what. I've seen acting students come and go; most of them don't have a chance in this business. They live on hope and they never make it, but they keep right on hoping, even when it should be obvious to them that they should give up and find something better to do with their lives. The gorgeous girls, they either get married to rich guys or become prostitutes. But you, you've got something special, and it's more than looks and a good, no great, body. I picked up on it the minute you walked into the room tonight."

I looked at him warily.

"I suppose it sounds like a line to you, but I really mean

it. You have star quality, as we call it here in Tinseltown."

"That's what my mother says," I replied, probably sounding pretty naive.

He smiled. "See? Your mother thinks it, and I think it. But we're not in a position to make you a star. She can give you encouragement, and I can teach you something about acting, but we can't get you parts."

I listened; what he was saying made sense.

"However," he went on, "if you stick with this, someday a big producer or director will pick up on your special quality, and they'll be able to do something for you."

Even though at this point in my life I wasn't dead set on becoming a successful entertainer, what he was saying made me feel very good. Who wouldn't, after all? It was all very flattering, especially to a poor kid from the slums of Saginaw, Michigan. For once in my young life I felt proud of myself, proud of what I had to offer.

"You keep coming to class twice a week," Tom told me, "and I'll teach you how to use your voice, how to present yourself. Stage presence or camera presence, as we call it here, shouldn't be too difficult for you to learn. Once you get over your self-consciousness you'll be great." He smiled. "For fourteen years old you do pretty good right now."

That, I knew, had to be a lie! But I liked him.

"Tom," I said, "my mother is really intent on starting me in an acting career. You seem to know the in's and out's of Hollywood and she doesn't. I'll bet she'd like to meet you."

"Fine," he replied, "I'd like to meet her."

"We live only a few blocks from here," I said. "Can you come over tomorrow, say around noon? We'll fix you a nice lunch and you and Mama can talk about my future stardom. I'll just listen."

He agreed, and I gave him our address. I said goodnight to Tom and walked out of the classroom, through the spic and span, shiny halls of Hollywood High, out into the cool Hollywood night.

I walked the few blocks home. It was only 10:45 and Mama wouldn't be coming for another hour-and-a-half, at least. It was such a nice meeting and I was in such a good mood that I decided to sit in the park across the street from our building for a few minutes to take it all in. After my conversation with Tom I felt relaxed and happy, infused with hope for a successful future and a good life in Hollywood.

The park was quiet, almost deserted, as I sat down on a bench and leaned back, relaxing and taking it all in. My head was filled with thoughts of bright lights and cool spring evenings, of having enough money to buy pretty clothes that I knew would look terrific on me; of having plenty of good food to eat; of going out in the evenings wearing diamond necklaces and all kinds of fine jewelry; of meeting a handsome man and falling in love and combining a successful career with a happy marriage. I was so wrapped up in my dreams that I didn't hear the sound behind me until it was too late.

A hand clamped roughly over my mouth and I froze.

"Just keep quiet, chickie, and you won't get hurt!" a man's voice said harshly. In the background, I could hear footsteps in the grass.

"Hey, nice piece of black ass," another man's voice came from where I had heard the footsteps.

I was terrified. I felt like my head was going to explode as something was tied around my eyes so that I couldn't see at all.

"Oh, God!" I thought, petrified with fear. "Not again! Why! Why!"

They began to drag me, I couldn't see where. Suddenly

I was furious. I began to kick and struggle.

"You better cool it, you black bitch!" a voice hissed, and I felt a sharp sting across my face, then another and another.

Moments later, I was down on the ground and I could hear the buttons popping off my blouse as they ripped it off me. I could feel the cloth over my eyes getting wet as the tears poured from my covered eyes. By now they had my mouth stuffed with something and my jaw ached. I could feel my lips beginning to swell.

"If only I could go home . . . Why, oh why did I ever come to this park . . . I never should have come here. . . ." The thoughts hammered through my head.

I heard myself groan as a sharp pain ripped through my groin.

"Open your legs, black bitch!" He kicked me again and I thought I would faint.

Then there were footsteps. "Freeze!"

"Cops," I thought, crying with relief. "It must be the cops . . ." But the voice sounded familiar.

The two men ran, but I didn't hear any gunfire. Then strong arms were lifting me, the gag was taken out of my dry mouth, and when the blindfold was removed I found myself face-to-face with Stan, the manager. He was half-smiling, kind of, but I could see the concern in his eyes.

"Boy, are you lucky I happened to come along," he said.

I burst into tears again.

"Hey, you're all right, aren't you? I got here in time, didn't I?" He really seemed to care.

"Yes," I sobbed, "you got here in time."

He bent over and picked up my torn blouse, then helped me put it on and I held it closed with my hand. I stopped crying, but my whole body was shaking.

"Is your mother home yet?" he asked. "There was no light on in your apartment when I went out fifteen minutes ago to get some beer." He held up a brown paper grocery bag, presumably with the beer in it.

"No," I said, "she gets home from work after midnight."

"Come on," he said, gently putting his arm around my shoulders, "I'll take you home and get you cleaned up. Your mother will be very upset if she sees you like this. What mother wouldn't be? Then we'll tell her about it, okay?"

"Okay," I said, still shaking.

We walked across the street to the apartment building. In front of my door, he took my purse and got my key out, then opened the door. Inside, he sat me down on the daybed and went into the bathroom, coming back out with a washcloth soaked in cold water. As he gently cleaned off my swollen face, I studied him. He was a fat man and not particularly handsome, but there was something so nice and tender about him, and he had warm, sensual eyes.

He went over to the closet and took out what he quickly determined was my bathrobe. He came back, laid it on the daybed, and removed my clenched hand from my torn blouse where I was still holding it closed.

"Come on, Mary Clarissa," he said, "you don't have to be afraid of me."

I let him take off the blouse, then expected him to put my bathrobe on. He didn't. What he did was unhook my bra with one hand; with the other he began to caress my breasts. I couldn't believe what was happening, yet I did nothing to stop him.

"Mary Clarissa," he whispered, "you're so beautiful." He removed my bra and tossed it on the daybed, on top of the robe. "I can't believe how beautiful you are."

He ran his fingers over my nipple, ever so gently, then kissed it, and I felt passion surging through my entire body. I wanted to make him stop, but I just didn't have the strength, physically or emotionally.

Soon he had all my clothes off, and I stood before him, totally nude. It was the first time a man had ever seen me this way, yet I was strangely calm. I enjoyed the way he looked at every part of my body, passionately, admiringly.

He took me in his arms, and soon we were lying on the daybed, wrapped up in each other. He had no clothes on either, and even though he was overweight and didn't have a good physique, he looked great to me. He showed me different ways to give him pleasure, and I couldn't believe what I was doing. Later, I would realize what a wonderful lover he was, but at this time I had no one to compare him with. I had never been with a man, except those terrible rapists in Saginaw, and in my mind, they didn't count. Rape is an act of hostility and violence, not sex as normal people experience sex.

We made love and at the last moment, he pulled out. I guess he wanted to be sure I didn't get pregnant. Afterward, as I slipped into my bathrobe, Stan opened one of the beers he had brought in.

He poured some for me in a glass. "Here," he said, handing it to me, "even though you're too young to have this, have some anyway."

"What do you mean, too young?" I asked, alarmed. Had he found out my real age? "I'm eighteen," I lied.

"Well, you have to be twenty-one to drink in California," he said. "Why? Is the drinking age younger in Michigan?"

"No, no," I laughed. "It's twenty-one there, too. I guess I just wasn't thinking." That was for sure, this whole evening had become unreal to me. First the acting class, which now seemed like ages ago; then the near disaster in the park; now this.

Stan got dressed, and not a moment too soon. A key turned, the door opened, and there was mother.

She looked at me, sitting on the daybed in my robe, and Stan, pouring himself another beer.

"Exactly what is going on here?" Mama asked tightly, walking into the apartment. Then she noticed my swollen face. "Oh, my God, baby, what happened to you?" she asked, quickly dismissing whatever wrong impression she had had.

"What almost happened would be more accurate," Stan explained, opening another beer and handing it to my mother. Stan told my mother what had happened in the park and how he had happened along and rescued me. She hugged me, relieved that I was all right. I wondered how she would react if she knew the last part of the story. What would she say if she knew that Stan and I had just had sex, right there on the daybed. I put the question out of my mind; I had no intention of telling her, and I was sure Stan wasn't going to either. After all, he was a married man.

Suddenly I remembered the time when I was a little child and I had walked in on my father having sex with a woman other than my mother, and how upset she had been. I felt a wave of shame come over me, but I put that out of my mind, too. What was the big deal? His wife would never find out, no one would. Later, I was to learn that Stan was making it with half the women, single and married alike, in the building, and a few in the next building as well. Why not? After all, he was a super terrific lover who obviously had enough to go around.

Mama excused herself and went into the bathroom, and Stan whispered to me, "Tell me, Mary Clarissa, am I as good as a black man?"

I looked at him, amazed. "I wouldn't know," I whispered back. "You're the first man, white or black, I've ever really been with."

Stan looked shocked. It would seem that someone with his experience could have figured it out, but he hadn't.

Stan left and Mama and I prepared for bed. But I couldn't sleep that night, except in fitful dozes. I couldn't shake my feelings of guilt for having gone to bed with a married man, although it had happened so fast I really didn't have time to consider. But extramarital affairs had caused much trouble in my parents' marriage, and I really didn't want to be the cause of any problems in anyone else's marriage.

It was beginning to turn light outside when I finally managed to fall asleep, promising myself that I would never do such a thing again. If it took two to tango, I would never again be one of the two.

CHAPTER 4

The next day, Tom, the acting coach, came over for lunch as we had planned, and I listened with half an ear as he and Mama discussed my presumably fabulous future and how to take the first steps to assure it. I had my mind on more immediate things, like what to do if Stan tried to make it with me again. Would I be able to resist? I didn't know, but I hoped so. And now that I wasn't afraid of guys and sex anymore — I had lost my fear so quickly that I wasn't even used to being without it yet — I wanted to meet boys my own age, black guys, to go out with like a normal girl of fourteen.

I kept attending Tom's acting workshop, and everyone said my skills as a performer were really improving.

'I don't know if you'll ever be a real actress," Tom told me, "but a performer you are!"

"What do you mean?" I asked him. "What's the difference?"

Tom laughed. "Well, Mary Clarissa, an actor has to be able to identify with a character. He has to sort of combine another person's psyche with his own, and to make believe that what is happening in the script is happening to him, really happening. He needs to make the audience suspend disbelief and really believe, for the moment, that what is happening on the screen or stage is true. It's a special talent, and I'm afraid it's not your strong point."

"Oh," I said, crestfallen but far from devastated. I wasn't that crazy about what he called acting anyway.

"Your best feature," Tom went on, "aside from your great face and fantastic body, is your personality, your charisma. Even when you're self-conscious, you're charming! I told you before, and I'll tell you again: you, my dear, have star quality."

"Star quality, fine," I said, "thank you for saying it. But how do I get parts?"

"Ah," said Tom ruefully, "in Hollywood, that is always the big question. How does an actor or actress get work?" It was a question to which he apparently had no answer.

He and my mother had gotten to be friends, platonic only, I'm sure, and he would come over during the day. Both of them would put me to work stapling my 8 x 10 glossies to my resume photocopies, then making up labels and mailing them out to agents and casting directors. My resume was a big joke — none of it was true. My only acting credit was Tom's workshop, and that went under "training." I had never even been in a school play. I was happy with my pictures, though, and looked at them whenever I felt a little depressed. I really looked sexy and gorgeous in my pictures, as everyone told me I did in person.

Finally, after countless interviews, I signed with an agent, a small-time agent out in the San Fernando Valley. He asked for fifty pictures and resumes, which he used to submit me to casting directors for various parts, but he only got me two interviews, and I didn't get either part.

"Look at it this way," Tom advised my mother. "She's not going to get anywhere with this agent, he has no clout. But she's got to hang in there until industry people get to know her; then she'll get a good agent and directors and producers will be asking for her. It's only a matter of time, Hattie, believe me."

I wondered why Tom took such an interest in my non-existent career. Perhaps it was because his own acting career was going no place, and he really believed I could be a star, in which case he would feel like he discovered me. Sometimes, I guess, vicarious enjoyment is better than none.

Mother and I also got to be friends with Stan and his wife, Mae. We were always going over there for coffee or drinks. They had a seven-year-old son who really was a little brat; he kept referring to us as "the coloreds" even though Stan and Mae scolded him for it. What did they expect, though? That was the way they referred to black people when we weren't around. I'm not sure they meant anything bad by it, though; they just seemed to be a bit ignorant. Incidentally, I solved the problem of Stan wanting to make it with me very easily one night when he came over and my mother was at work.

I let him come in, and I sat down provocatively on the daybed. Before he could come near me, though, I blurted out, "Stan, I think there's something I should tell you. I'm fourteen-years-old."

I thought he was going to pass out.

"Jail bait!" he muttered, white as a sheet.

I couldn't resist being facetious. "I hope it doesn't change anything between us," I said demurely.

"What?" he replied, then hastily added, "no, no, of course not. Why would it change anything?"

But he never came near me again, although I could see he was still very attracted to me. Both those things were just fine with me.

Once when my mother and I were visiting at Stan and Mae's apartment, some friends of theirs dropped over, and during the course of the conversation Mae brought up the story of how Stan rescued me from the rapists in the park. I could see Stan becoming uncomfortable, his mind probably filled with what happened afterward, which he never wanted anyone to find out.

". . . and then he yelled, 'Freeze,' " Mae said, "and the two creeps high-tailed it out of there, right fast, too."

Suddenly I realized there was something I had been meaning to ask Stan, yet never had.

"Stan," I said, "I never did find out why they ran when you yelled 'freeze.' Did you have a gun, or what?"

Stan smiled knowingly, and so did his wife. Suddenly he jumped up, pulled something out of his pocket, and assumed a threatening position, holding it with both hands.

"Freeze!" he shouted, and instinctively, we all did, even Mae.

Then he burst out laughing, tossing the "weapon" on the floor. Clearly, it was a toy, a little black plastic pistol that didn't even look real from where I was sitting. I began to realize what Tom had meant about acting. Anyone would have thought that Stan was holding a real gun, but only because of his actions and the way he handled it. I don't think I ever could have brought anything like that across, acting lessons or not!

"Stan," I teased, "are you sure you're not an actor?"

"Nah," he replied, "I'm no actor. I'm a musician, and a damn good one at that. If only I could get some work." It was the eternal cry of people trying to make it in Hollywood, it seemed.

Stan got out his saxophone and gave us a little solo concert, and he really was quite good, I thought.

One evening when I was home alone and feeling a bit lonely, I decided to go over and visit Mae and Stan. "Stan's not home," Mae said as I walked in. "He took Junior to a flick on Hollywood Boulevard, some kind of Chinese fighting movie they both wanted to see. It's good to get 'em both out of my hair once in a while, I'll tell you that."

I smiled.

"Sit down, hon. I'll make us a pot of coffee," Mae offered.

We were sitting there sipping our coffee and chatting, when all of a sudden she said, "You know, Stan and I don't have a very good sex relationship."

I panicked. Had she found out that once I had gone to bed with him? No, I told myself, how could she? Besides, I already knew that her husband was making it with a good percentage of the females in the neighborhood, not to mention this very building.

I just shrugged, a little embarrassed.

"I hope you don't mind my running off at the mouth," Mae went on, "but I don't get out of the house much. But you're such a beautiful girl, and you got some body on you, too."

It was an odd thing for her to say to me, and I was really getting very uncomfortable. When she got up to get some more coffee, I felt strangely relieved.

She came back with the coffee and poured it, then opened a cabinet drawer and took out a small bottle of brandy, which she poured in her cup and mine.

"It's a good drink," she said, "coffee and brandy. Makes you feel relaxed all over."

I didn't like the way she was looking at me. I gulped down my coffee and brandy, even though it was too hot to drink that fast and she had put quite a bit of brandy in it. When I stood up, I felt a little dizzy.

"Well, I'd better be getting home now, Mae," I said politely.

"Oh, don't rush off," she smiled at me. "Come back in here and we can visit a while."

She took my hand firmly in hers and began to lead me toward the bedroom. When I tried to pull my hand away, she drew up real close to me, rubbing against my breasts. Then she began to caress my ass.

"Mae!" I exclaimed. "Stop it! What do you think you're doing?" It was a foolish question; it was obvious what she was doing.

"Silly child," she said. "Don't you know that another woman can satisfy you much better than any man?" She smiled seductively. "I found that out a long time ago. Men are okay too, of course, but . . ."

By this time, I was at the door, ready to run out. I had heard of lesbians and bisexual women, but I'd never met one that I knew of, and I didn't want any part of it.

"Mae," I interrupted her, "I think you're a very nice person, but I don't like you in the way you're saying. And I think I'll leave right now."

I rushed out, leaving her standing there. I ran back to my apartment and locked the door, using both top and bottom lock. Then I fastened the chain.

I wondered what made her think I would be interested in going to bed with her. I didn't know too much about homosexuality, but later on I was told by a sophisticated friend that she probably just had the hots for me, and since I was so young, thought that maybe I could learn to enjoy sex with women as well as with men. After all, apparently that was her bag. But as far as I was concerned, I didn't want any part of it.

"Oh, how I wish I could just meet a nice black dude and fall in love," I thought, almost wishing I were back in our old neighborhood in Saginaw, slummy and filthy though it was. (It's so easy to romanticize a terrible place once you're not there anymore, and I guess I'm basically a born romantic.) At least, I thought, in Saginaw there were some good-looking, eligible, sexy black bucks; although most of them were roughnecks and jerks, there must have been some nice guys. Here in Hollywood, young and gorgeous though I was, I was having trouble establishing a love life. Little did I know that my problem would soon be over, that soon I would have more love life than I could handle.

Also, I decided to say nothing about Mae's overtures toward me; she and Stan were good friends with Mama and me. And soon, although I didn't know it then, Mae and Stan would indirectly play an important role in changing the course of my life, forever.

CHAPTER 5

Time passed and soon I realized that my life in Hollywood had become routine. I was beginning to become bored, my whole young being crying out for some excitement. Mama still had her waitress job at the restaurant; they had given her two raises already and she said the tips were very good.

"Well, you're a good waitress, Mama," I told her with pride.

"Big deal," Mama laughed, but I knew she really took pride in her work. That's the kind of woman she was.

"You know, Mama," I said, "I've been thinking. Maybe it's time I went out and got a job myself."

"A job?" she exclaimed. "I'll hear of no such thing. You have a career to think of!"

"Oh, what career, Mama?" I replied sadly. "I haven't made one penny as an actress yet."

"But between your agent and me and Tom, we've been getting you auditions," she pointed out. "Why, remember we went to that producer's office just the other day . . ."

"Sure, Mama," I said bitterly. "And the bastard tried to screw me on his red velvet couch while you were sitting out in the reception room waiting! But he sure didn't say anything about any part."

Mama was silent for a few moments, then she began

slowly, "Hon, of course he didn't say anything about any part. You didn't do anything to please him, did you?"

I was surprised. "Of course not, Mama. Are you nuts, or what?"

"No, I'm not nuts," she said slowly. "You're not a little girl anymore, honey, and if that's the way it's done in Hollywood . . ."

I covered my ears with my hands. I didn't want to hear any of it.

"So maybe you should consider . . ."

"No!" I shouted. "There's no way I'm going to screw some old fart of a producer just on the chance that he *may* give me some dinky little part in his stupid ol' movie."

"Honey, I didn't say you should; I just said that maybe you should consider it, think about it," my mother said tactfully.

"No way!" I yelled, then grabbed my purse and ran out of the apartment.

I got onto Sunset Boulevard and began to walk. I needed to walk, to burn off some of my energy, my boredom and frustration. And I needed to think. What the hell was I doing in Hollywood? Where was my life going? No place, it seemed.

I walked along, it must have been for a good three miles, and I soon found myself in the Sunset Strip area. I wasn't dressed up, just wearing jeans and a plain blouse, but I couldn't walk a block without guys calling out to me from passing cars.

"Hey, pretty lady, want a ride?" was one of the more polite invitations. What some of them said, I wouldn't even repeat. There were so many different approaches these guys used to "introduce themselves" to a girl, and all the approaches led to the same place, as far as I could see — bed. Right then, I wasn't the least bit interested in any of them. In fact, I was so used to being approached that a lot of the time I didn't even take any notice.

The Sunset Strip area was a lot more fashionable section than the part of Sunset Boulevard where we lived, and soon I found myself window shopping in some of the expensive boutiques. The clothes were simply gorgeous. How nice it would be to be able to afford to walk into a boutique, pick out half a dozen dresses and pant suits, put it all on a credit card and walk out, without batting an eye. I stood there and watched as some women did just that.

"And most of them are not half as pretty as me," I thought. "How do they do it?" Well, I had a pretty good idea of how some of them did it, but I didn't want to think about that.

My legs were beginning to ache from the long walk, and I had some change on me so I decided to take a bus and go home. Either that or I would go to the Hollywood library, where I spent a good deal of my time, believe it or not. I may not have realized it at the time, but I was getting back in school in Saginaw. I would just sit there and read books on all kinds of subjects: art, literature, history, books about animals, books about different cultures. I found all of it interesting, and if there was something I didn't understand, I asked the librarian, who was always very helpful. And at the library, at least in those days, there weren't any creeps hanging around. Now, it may be different; I don't know. I don't go to the Hollywood library anymore; I don't have to.

The bus came and I got on and took a seat. From where I was sitting, I soon noticed that the driver, a clean-cut looking black guy, was staring at me through the rear view mirror. When he noticed that I was looking back at him, he smiled, but I turned away and looked out the window. I just wasn't in any mood for attention, no matter how complimentary, from men.

Pretty soon, the bus stopped a half block from the famous Schwab's drug store, and I got off. I was still a good distance from home, but I really didn't feel like going home to face my mother. I needed to cool off. I realized that she meant well and wanted the best for me, but I was disgusted at her suggestion. I realized that she, as a woman, could never do what she was telling me to do. And I just wasn't that desperate at the time to get parts.

"I'll see her when she gets home from work tonight," I thought. "Then we can talk it out." One thing about my mother, we could always talk a thing out. It was one of my favorite qualities about her.

I walked into Schwab's and sat down at the famous counter where Lana Turner was supposedly "discovered."

"What'll you have?" the waitress asked, wiping off the counter.

"Coke, lots of ice," I told her.

The waitress smiled. "But hon, if I put a lot of ice in it, you'll be getting less Coke. Waste of money, if you ask me."

I hadn't. I shrugged and said, "Then charge me less, or give me two of them." There was nothing shy about me anymore.

She thought what I said was very funny. "Can't do it, hon," she replied. "I'd get fired in a hurry."

"Then don't do it," I replied, studying her. She was middle-aged and slightly overweight, with big boobs. Her face looked as though at one time, she had been beautiful. When had she come to Hollywood, I wondered. Twenty, thirty years ago? I had seen pictures at the library of Hollywood in the '30s and '40s. It wasn't as built up then, and it didn't look as crowded. The hairstyles were very different, as were the fashions in clothing, and the automobiles were quaint.

"But I'll bet it was the same as far as getting parts in movies," I thought sardonically. "That's probably never changed, and never will."

I wondered if the waitress had come here to be a star and ended up waitressing at Schwab's, instead of being discovered there. If so, she didn't seem unhappy.

"Are you an actress?" I asked her as she neatly set a napkin and a glass of Coca Cola in front of me.

Her whole face brightened up. "Why, yes," she replied, "though goodness knows it's been a long time since anyone's asked me that question!"

"Did you ever get any acting work?" I asked, though I realized it was a tactless question. It was just the mood I was in.

Her face clouded over and I felt guilty for having lifted her up and dropped her back down.

But she had dignity. "Once in a while I do a play," she said. "There's not very much money in plays, but it's acting, it's art. I'm an actress, and I have to act, right?"

I nodded my agreement, although I really didn't understand what the hell was so damned important about acting. Then I saw a flicker of hope come into her eyes.

"I did a couple of movies, years ago, and I've still kept up my Screen Actors Guild dues. You see, I have an agent whom I just signed with a few months ago, and he thinks he can get me auditions for parts on television. Situation comedy, you know, they're looking for my type, he says. And commercials, maybe he can get me a couple of those. Boy, one commercial and all those residuals and I could quit my job here, that's for sure."

I smiled. "How long have you been working here?" I asked.

"Oh, not too long," she replied offhandedly, but I got the feeling she had been working there for a very long time. Either there, or maybe at Denny's, or MacDonalds, or somewhere like that. Still, she thought she had a career in show business. It was amazing to me how people in Hollywood could fool themselves. I hoped whatever they had wasn't catching!

I finished my Coke and walked all the way home from Schwab's, a little over a mile, I guess. When I got in the apartment, Mama had already gone to work, as I'd hoped. I fixed myself some pan-fried potatoes and a hamburger, which I ate without enthusiasm. My life, my values were all mixed up; I had a lot to sort out.

CHAPTER 6

One evening at Tom's acting class, a new student walked into the classroom. I had been studying my lines for the scene I was supposed to do with another actress, so I didn't notice him until he plopped himself down next to me.

"Hi!" he said in a friendly manner. "My name's William Jones. What's yours?"

He was a light-complected black guy, about 19, with a sensitive face and manner. He had dark, sensual eyes, and I liked his friendly but not overly aggressive personality. He was a good-looking dude.

"My name's Mary Clarissa Stevens," I replied, "but I can't talk with you now." I pointed to the script in front of me. "Gotta study my lines, you know?"

"Sure," he said, and switched his seat a few rows over. But he kept looking back at me and I lost my concentration on my lines. Some actress I was!

Tom asked him to stand up and introduce himself, then instructed William Jones to come up to the front of the room and read a scene with him. Tom did this "test of fire," as he called it, to all new acting students. As William walked up to the front, I noticed that he was even more attractive than I had originally thought. He was very tall, about 6'4", and lanky but muscular. And he had a very relaxed, manly walk.

William read a scene from "Zoo Story" by Edward Albee, where he, William, had most of the lines and Tom just reacted to him. William read so well that he received spontaneous applause, another plus for him in my book!

On the break, about halfway through the class, I began a conversation with a group of students, carefully positioning myself to be in clear view of William whom, I noticed, was watching me. I spoke in the sexiest voice I could muster. Acting lessons hadn't been a complete waste of time, after all! Then I excused myself from the group and walked off to the water fountain in the hallway, making it easy for William to come over and talk to me.

He picked up his cue. "Hi again, Mary Clarissa," he said, approaching me. "When's your big scene coming up?"

I smiled seductively, although as I look back at it now, I really didn't have to try to be sexy. I guess I didn't have as much self-confidence as I do now.

"It's coming next," I told him. "But I'm really not much of an actress. I'm just a beautiful, sexy girl, who the teacher says it going to be a star someday!" I said it lightly with a big smile, so as not to appear conceited. But conceited I was getting to be, I guess.

"I agree with that wholeheartedly," William replied. "Especially about your being beautiful and sexy. But nobody knows who's going to be a star, not in Hollywood."

I agreed. I could see William was a realist, like myself. Another plus for William.

"That was a nice reading you did," I complimented him, but coolly, not wanting to appear too anxious. "You're a good actor, for a student."

"Thank you, Mary Clarissa," he said. "I was very nervous."

That surprised me. "You sure didn't seem to be," I told him sincerely.

He shrugged. "I've learned to cover it up. All actors get nervous."

"I know, I know," I laughed. "Even what's-her-name, the famous great actress, throws up before a performance."

"Helen Hayes is her name," he said, "and I'm not sure if I believe all that!"

We both laughed and started back to the classroom.

He looked like he wanted to say something, and then he did. "Mary Clarissa, would you like to go out for coffee with me after class?" He had a fine, deep voice and such flawless diction that I wondered what the hell he was doing in an acting class at Hollywood High. Little did I know that many very experienced actors still attend classes, just to keep their craft in shape. Boy, I could never do that. Once I learn something, that's it. No more classes for me! Trouble was, I still needed acting classes.

I hesitated at his question. "Well, I don't know, I do have to get home . . ."

"It's up to you," he smiled. "But I won't keep you out late. We can have some coffee and pie, and then I'll drive you right home. Do you live far from here?" He had such a relaxed, easy manner.

"No, I live close by, just a couple of blocks away, and I usually walk home."

"Well, Mary Clarissa, have coffee with me after class, and tonight you'll ride home in style, that is, if you don't mind a beat-up old Volkswagen."

He was so nice. "Okay, William," I agreed. "But we won't stay out too late."

He looked overjoyed. "You got it!" he agreed, then put

his arm around my shoulder and we walked back into the classroom.

My scene, which was from "Streetcar Named Desire" by Tennessee Williams, was a disaster. The actor whom I did it with was a gay black guy who had no idea of how to portray Stanley with the toughness and macho attitude the part required. At the end of the scene, he's supposed to start raping me, which was probably why Tom assigned us the scene. He thought I still had problems due to my being raped, but I didn't. The scene was terrible and a complete waste of time. Besides, thanks to William being in the audience, I had absolutely no concentration, forgot half my lines and delivered the other half of them to William instead of the actor with whom I was working, the way I was supposed to. I was terrible, but still everyone paid attention to me, the way people always did. I was beginning to thank God for my looks, figure and good personality, but I didn't think I had one iota of talent in those days. And you know what? In those days, I didn't much care, although I probably should have, at least a little.

After class, William and I went to the Copper Penny restaurant on La Brea and Sunset Boulevard, and sat and talked for more than two hours over coffee and apple pie. He was in a quiet mood, it seemed, but I was really turned on. I kept the conversation going with all kinds of anecdotes about my ridiculous experiences in Hollywood. At times, I noticed other people in the coffee shop looking over at me, and I was glad. I guess by then I had become a "natural" performer.

"And so," I laughed, "now I've been here over four years, and now I'm *really* eighteen, but I feel more like twenty-two, because I told people I was eighteen when I was only fourteen. Are you getting all this?" I asked William.

He said, "I sure am, babe!"

"I don't know how you could be!" I exclaimed, still laughing.

"Well, if I'm not," he smiled, "I'm sure having fun listening to you. You're like a black female Johnny Carson, but of course much sexier," he added.

"Oh, wow!" I replied. "Just what the networks want! A black female Johnny Carson, but much sexier! If I'm so great, how come I ain't rich?!"

"I don't know," he said pensively. "How come I ain't either?"

William looked nineteen, but he was twenty-five, and he had been an actor since the age of fifteen. He had worked in theater a lot, touring the country in a fine production of "Othello." He had even worked in New York, not on Broadway, but Off Broadway, and that was more than a lot of actors had done. Before that, he had done all kinds of summer stock.

"I quit school at fifteen," he told me, "but I educated myself, at least in theater. Theater, acting, that's my church, my religion," William said with passion.

I skirted the issue of love for acting, of which I had very little. "You might say "I'm self-educated, too," I told him, explaining my interest in just about every subject, and my voracious reading.

"Well, it's nice to see a gorgeous chick who's also intelligent," he said, "but I'd never take you for a book worm!" He reached out and touched my hand, there on the table. "You know, Mary Clarissa, I think I'm falling in love with you. And I don't do that number very often."

I looked into his deep brown eyes and realized that he meant what he was saying. He was so nice, so good-looking, just the kind of guy I had been hoping for so long to meet. But even in his gentle way, he was moving too fast for me.

I looked at my watch, the Timex my mother had saved up and bought me for Christmas as a surprise.

"Oh, my God!" I nearly shrieked. "It's after one in the morning. Mama will be worried sick; I never stay out late without at least calling her and telling her I'm all right!"

William looked around. "There's a phone right over there. Want to call her and let her know you're on your way home?"

"No, no," I said, getting up. "Let's just get out of here. I've got to get home; it's only a few minutes away."

William left a small tip and paid the check, and we got into his little old VW bug and drove to my place. The light was on and I could see Mama looking out the window as William pulled over to the curb and parked right in front of the apartment building.

"My mother's watching," I said. "Would you like to come in for a minute and meet her? Or do you have to be up early in the morning?"

"I'd love to meet her," he replied, flashing his delightful smile. "I do have to be up early; I work in a warehouse downtown. But thanks to you, Mary Clarissa, I'm wide awake."

We walked in and Mama's concern vanished the moment she met William. She liked him instantly.

"I'm sorry for keeping Mary Clarissa out so late and worrying you, Mrs. Stevens, but . . ."

Mama interrupted him. "My goodness!" she exclaimed. "Old-fashioned good manners and politeness! I thought it had vanished in this world of 1972. But never you mind, William," she went on, "Mary Clarissa should have known better and called me. Anyway, this is the first time one of her boyfriends has ever been so polite."

"Mama!" I exclaimed. "Now don't start giving away my secrets!" The secret was, I didn't have any real boyfriends, because I very rarely accepted any dates.

"Of course," Mama agreed, smiling. "Now, I'll fix us some coffee."

"Never mind, Mama," I told her. "We've been drinking

coffee all evening. I'll put on some water for tea. How's that?"

"Fine with me," said William, gazing at me. He really was turned on, in his quiet way.

We all sat and chatted for another hour, then William excused himself. I walked him outside, where he took me in his arms and kissed me goodnight. He had a wonderful, tender, exciting touch and I kissed him back, hard.

"Can I see you tomorrow night?" he asked, breathing hard. "I haven't even gone yet, and I miss you already."

"Well, tomorrow night I'm busy," I lied.

He didn't say anything.

"But Friday night would be fine," I added, not wanting to miss the opportunity of seeing him again.

"I'm in a play reading on Friday night, with the acting group I belong to," he said. "But if you'd like to come to the reading, we can go out afterward for a late supper. What do you say?"

I pretended to think about it, though I knew full well that my answer would be an emphatic "Yes!" I hated to play games, but Mama had always emphasized that this was the way it was done, and I didn't want to take any chances. Meeting someone I really liked didn't happen to me every day or every year, for that matter.

William smiled, and I suspect now that he knew what I was up to, though I didn't realize it then. He had really been around.

"Come on now, babe," he said, still smiling, "I guarantee it's not that bad a play, though it's an original we're reading. And I have the lead part."

"All right," I said, "it's a date."

"I'll pick you up at 6:30," he said, then took me in his arms and we kissed again.

I could feel the passion welling up inside me, and I broke away from him and rushed into the apartment. He must have stood there waiting for me to get inside, because as I stood leaning against the door, my face flushed with passion, I didn't hear his car start up until a few moments later. I fantasized making love with him in that little car. I don't know why. I had never done anything like that before or even thought about it. The guy really turned me on.

Mama went about, opening the daybed, winding the alarm clock, preparing for bed, pretending not to notice me and the state I was in.

Finally I rushed over to her.

"Mama," I said, "isn't he something else? I mean, isn't he simply wonderful?!"

"Yes," she replied, "he's a very nice young man, and I can see he really likes you and respects you." But something was wrong, I could tell.

"Mama, what is it?" I asked, perplexed.

She stopped what she was doing and sat down on the partially-made daybed.

"I know you're going to think your old Mama is not a very nice person, or very romantic for that matter. But that was the way I felt the first time I met your father, just the way you're feeling right now." She had a faraway look in her eyes, and then I could see tears starting to form. "And look at the way it turned out. So badly, so badly."

I became very upset. "Stop it, Mama!" I yelled. "That's a terrible thing to say!" I waved my finger in her face. "And you had some pretty good times with him, you said that yourself. You should be grateful for that!"

She just sat there, looking sad, and I felt sorry for shouting at her.

"Mama," I said softly, "it doesn't have to be that way for me, and besides, everything would have been fine with you and Papa, if it hadn't been for the accident." Damn that accident, I thought. My whole life would have been different, too, if it hadn't been for that damned accident.

Why did God have to do things like that to people, I thought contemptuously. "God loves you," they had taught in Sunday School when I was a little kid. Sure He does, I thought now, sure. And so does Santa Claus, and so does the Tooth Fairy.

Suddenly my mother grabbed my hands, both of them, and held them tightly in hers. When she spoke, there was an intensity in her voice that I had never heard before. "Mary Clarissa, my baby," she said, "I wanted so much more for you. If you keep seeing that boy, nine chances out of ten you'll end up marrying him."

I pulled my hands away. "What would be so terrible about that?" I hissed, trying to hold back the tears I felt coming on.

"If you marry him, or someone like him, no matter how nice he is, no matter how much he loves you, you'll just be an ordinary woman, like everyone else. You're special, Mary Clarissa, *special!*" She said the word with the awe and intensity one usually reserves for worship. "And the world must know how special you are! Do you understand me, Mary Clarissa, do you?"

I was taken completely aback. My mother had become a fanatic, and it frightened me.

"Mama," I said softly, looking away, "please let's talk about it tomorrow. I'm very tired and all I want to do is go to sleep. Is that okay?"

Suddenly all the fire went out of her; her shoulders drooped and all the expressiveness went out of her face. She looked tired and worn out, and I felt sorry for her.

"Come on, Mama," I said gently. "Let's get some sleep."

But I couldn't sleep; I never could sleep when I had an important matter on my mind. I guess it's a form of insomnia. I read for most of the night, a romantic novel about Mary, Queen of Scots.

CHAPTER 7

William and I went out that Friday night, and we had a good time. But there was a cloud hanging over me, and it was because of my mother's crazy values. At least, that was the way I saw it. Her attitude was wrong, and it disturbed me deeply, because I loved her very much, and probably because I didn't yet have complete confidence in my own values.

William, sensitive soul that he was, sensed that something was wrong. We sat sipping wine in his cheaply but cozily furnished apartment in Silver Lake, a middle class area south of Hollywood.

"Was the play reading that boring?" he joked.

I touched his hand. "No, no, William, it wasn't boring at all, not in the least. And you did such a fabulous reading. It wasn't like you were reading, or even acting. It was like you were really that person who you were portraying, and every scene you were in seemed like it was really happening. You really did an excellent job." And he really had. William was a fabulous actor, probably a gifted actor. "The world should know how really special you are." I bit my tongue as I realized I had repeated my mother's very words.

"You're sweet," he said tenderly.

He took me in his arms and I yielded to him. His very touch sent spasms of ecstasy through me as he gently undressed me. Then he took his own clothes off, and his body was lithe and muscular. He moved like a panther, and his every movement excited me.

"You're beautiful," he whispered, taking me into his arms again. "You're the most beautiful woman I've ever seen, the most beautiful woman in the world . . ."

He took me into his bed, throwing back the covers quickly as we slipped into bed together. I felt completely protected in his strong arms. His voice, his every movement, drove me wilder and wilder with excitement as we made mad, passionate love. Yet just as I was about to reach orgasm, I turned off. I pretended, but he saw through my act. Remember, I wasn't a very good actress.

He sat up in bed, leaning against the worn wooden headboard.

"What is it, Mary Clarissa? Did I do something to turn you off?"

"No, William, of course not! Nothing could be further from the truth," I told him sincerely. I knew what it was, the argument with my mother. Did I dare tell him about that? I was ridden with guilt, first about the disagreement with my mother, then about spoiling everything with William. What the hell is wrong with me, I thought. I'm eighteen years old, a grown woman, not a little five-year-old girl who needs her mother's approval for everything!

"I realize we know each other for such a short time," William was saying. "But it doesn't seem like it to me. I love you, Mary Clarissa, I really do."

I moved close to him. "It seems to me we've known each other forever," I said, and I meant it. "And I think I love you, too." The hell with my mother and her game playing. "The problem is, my mother thinks I should look for a man who can help me with my career; she thinks I'm supposed to be a big star or something. That's what she wants and although she likes you, she doesn't think you're the right one for me." I spilled it all out, afraid to look at him, scared of what his reaction would be. "And I know I'm being ridiculous and silly and childish; after all, I'm eighteen years old and I don't need my mother's sanction for anything I do, but . . ."

William gently covered my mouth with his hand. Automatically, I looked into his eyes. They were happy.

"Mary Clarissa, Mary Clarissa," he said, "if that's all it is, you don't have a thing to worry bout — *we* don't have a thing to worry about. It's a perfectly normal reaction, and you'll get over it. Just you listen to me."

I moved his hand down slightly so I could talk. I still felt the need to explain. "You see," I said, "my mother and I have been very close, always, and I was so shocked to find out that she felt that way . . ."

He burst out laughing, then took me in his arms and made love to me again. Again, it was ecstasy, but still I couldn't reach orgasm, as much as I desperately wanted to.

Still, William was undisturbed. "You're trying too hard, babe. But that will go away, in time."

We got out of bed and William poured us some wine, which we sat sipping for about an hour, talking, smiling at each other.

"Come on, baby" he said finally, "time to take you home."

We rode back to Hollywood in silence; no words were necessary. We were enjoying each other's company, just being together in his car.

Again, he was able to get a parking space in front of my apartment, which faced the street. He kept the motor running while we kissed goodnight.

"I'll wait here in the car until I see your door close and know you're safely inside," he said. "And I'll see you in class on Wednesday."

"Okay," I said sullenly. He hadn't asked me for another date. Hell, I thought, I've screwed everything up!

"Now about next weekend . . ." he said, and my heart began to pound. "Have you ever been to Santa Barbara?"

I shook my head.

"It's a two-hour drive, and beautiful, along the coast. That's where we'll go, if it's all right with you."

"Yes," I said happily, without hesitation. No more game playing for me.

We kissed goodnight again, then I got out of the car and walked slowly up the walkway to the apartment door, turning around a couple of times, waving at William sitting there behind the driver's seat, blowing him a kiss.

I opened the door with my key, hoping my mother was asleep. She was. I went to bed and slept like a baby, having two different dreams about William, or was it three? I don't remember, but I woke up early in the morning more happy and refreshed than I'd been in a long time. I was in love.

I didn't have anymore problems with my mother; apparently she had decided to accept my decision to run my life the way I saw fit, whether it agreed with her views or not. I knew she was still disappointed in me, but because of her tolerant and accepting attitude, I could handle her disappointment.

William and I left early that Saturday morning, just a little after 6:30 a.m., and set out for the coastal town of Santa Barbara, around 90 miles from Hollywood. We took the scenic route along the coast, and it was so picturesque and beautiful. On our left, the sun sparkled over the great Pacific Ocean, and on our right we could view the rugged Southern California hills towering high above us in the little Volkswagen. Most important, I was with William and I was happy, free of conflicts, just enjoying the sunny, balmy day.

When we got to Santa Barbara, we drove along State Street, the main drag there, and stopped at a Mexican cafe in the El Paseo for a brunch of *huevos rancheros*, eggs with a zesty Mexican sauce.

"That was wonderful," I said, after we'd finished eating and sat sipping our coffee. I leaned back in the chair, full to the brim. "And the ride up here was beautiful — so romantic."

"Yes," said William, "nature has been good to this part of the country."

I smiled and nodded.

He leaned forward and took my hand. "I have a surprise for you, Mary Clarissa."

"You do?" I couldn't imagine what it could be.

"Yes," he said.

"Well, what is it?!" I loved surprises.

"This might sound corny, but you know the old adage about the best things in life being free?"

I nodded.

"Like the beautiful drive we just took."

I nodded again, becoming impatient. "Come on," I said, "come on! The suspense is killing me!"

"Well," he went on slowly, "that adage is only partially true. Some of the best things do cost money."

"William," I said, "what in the world are you talking about?"

He reached into his pocket and pulled out a crisp one hundred dollar bill.

I looked at him, confused.

"It's my whole savings account, just about."

"Huh?" I asked, now really confused.

"We're going to spend it enjoying ourselves here today and tomorrow, too, if you say 'yes.' We can rent a hotel room with a view, right on the beach, and go to a fabulous place for dinner, and I can buy you a present."

"A present?" I repeated dumbly.

"An engagement present," he said softly, "but again, only if you say 'yes.' Mary Clarissa, will you marry me?"

I was thunderstruck and I just sat there staring at him. "Yes," I said impulsively, tears coming to my eyes. "Yes, yes, yes!"

We left the restaurant and drove about a mile to the beach, where we sat on the sand holding hands, enjoying each other's company, watching the rhythmic motion of the water as it beat against the shore. We talked about our future together, making plans.

"About a year," William said, "that's how long it will take me to get in financial shape, then we can get married. I can start putting away money, maybe look for a better job. And I can look for a better agent, step on the gas as far as my acting career is concerned."

"You should do that, about your acting I mean," I told him. "You're such a good actor, there's no reason why you can't get work."

He smiled ruefully. "There aren't enough parts for the number of good actors in Hollywood, and that applies even more to black actors. But I'll never give up," he added with intensity. "With me, acting comes first, after you, that is, Mary Clarissa. You're number one in my life."

He was number one in my life, too. "Well," I said, "I'm going to get a job, that's what I'm going to do, and I can put money away, too. There's no reason why you should have to shoulder the whole money burden. This is 1972, not 1952, and I assume you've heard of the Women's Liberation Movement."

"Of course," he smiled. "And I would agree with it completely if all the women who burned their bras had figures like you!"

"Very funny!" I laughed, hugging him.

"Honestly, though," he said, "you're really a gem. But

if you get a job and start doing things like that, what about your acting career?"

"Hah!" I exclaimed. "What acting career? In Hollywood, I guess, I'm just another pretty face, another tits-and-ass small-town girl trying to make it big."

"No," he said seriously, "don't you ever talk like that. You're special, Mary Clarissa, a very special person, and don't you forget it."

"I only want to be special to one person," I answered. "And that person is you."

He kissed me, and it seemed that my dream of stardom, which had been my mother's dream in the first place, had faded away, belonging to a long gone past. So it seemed on that bright, sunny Saturday afternoon on the beach in Santa Barbara.

The weekend flew by, and Sunday evening we were back in Hollywood. The announcement of our engagement was not met with enthusiasm by my mother, but she was gracious and accepted it, even taking us out to a French restaurant on Franklin Avenue for a celebration dinner of crepes and wine.

Six months quickly passed by, and William and I were more in love than ever. They were such happy days we shared. I enjoyed every moment of those times, not realizing for a moment how complicated and conflict-ridden my life was soon to become.

CHAPTER 8

It was one of those rare rainy nights in L.A. when everyone says, "Great, we really need the water," even as they stand on the shoulder of the freeway next to their open-hooded, stalled automobiles.

William now had a slightly better job in the mailroom of one of the studios. He had been asked to work overtime on this rainy Friday night, after which he was going to pick me up and we would go to his place and watch "Treasure of the Sierra Madre," a grand old movie with Humphrey Bogart, on his black and white television.

I had taken a job as salesgirl in a five-and-ten on Hollywood Boulevard. I hated the job, but I loved the paycheck I got every week, which I promptly put into the savings account I had opened at a Bank of America branch across the street from work. My nest egg was building up; my mother wouldn't take a cent of my pay, even to help her with household expenses.

"You'll need every bit of it for when you and William get married," she said simply, and I could tell that she was still tremendously disappointed about my plans. But now I considered that her problem, not mine. I no longer felt guilty about her disapproval, and my original sex problem with William had long since vanished. My relationship with my future husband was getting better and better all the time, sexually and in every other way, having already surpassed the point of perfection.

In any event, on this rainy Friday night, I had just stepped out of a hot shower, and I sneezed several times.

"Damn!" I said aloud. I had been feeling badly all day, like I was coming down with a miserable cold.

I fixed a cup of hot herbal tea, and just as I was adding the honey, the telephone rang.

"Hi, babe," William said. "Bad news. Car won't start."

"Is the battery dead?" I asked. It seemed that when it rained, half the cars in L.A. wouldn't start.

"Naw," he answered, "I thought it was that at first, but now I think it's worse. I'll have my friend Phil come look at it, you know, the one who works in the gas station. I tried calling him, but he's not home and he's not at work. Guess I'll have to take the bus over to pick you up."

"The bus?" I interrupted. The so-called rapid transit bus system in Los Angeles is bad enough during the day; at night, it's hopeless. "You're over a mile from the nearest bus stop, and you'll have to take two buses to get here. It's nine o'clock now; by the time you get here it'll be . . ."

"I know," he said, "it'll be after 11:30. Maybe I should spring for a cab."

"It's up to you," I said. "But you don't know how much it's going to cost to fix the car." Since we were saving to get married, I had really become a miser, with my own money and his as well.

"You're right, babe," he said. "We'll just have to see each other tomorrow. Oh, hell, I'm really disappointed."

"So am I," I told him. "But I don't know how good company I'd be tonight anyway. It's miserable out and I feel like I'm coming down with some kind of flu or something. I'll see you tomorrow, as soon as you get the car fixed."

"I love you," he said softly.

"I love you, too," I told him, and hung up, already regretting my decision. Damn, I thought, just like an old lady, afraid to go out in the rain, saving money, complaining about a stupid cold. I almost called him back, but decided to leave things be. Later, I would consider this the biggest mistake I ever made, but now I just curled up in a chair, still in my robe, and began to read some boring magazine or other.

Soon, my mother came in, soaking wet.

"No date?" she asked brightly. She was probably hoping that William and I had broken up.

"His car won't start," I muttered, my face still in the magazine.

"Well," she said, "no point in staying home alone. Mae and Stan and I are going out; why don't you come along with us?"

"Nah," I said bluntly.

"But it'll be fun. Stan's going to play at a jazz club on Western Avenue. Come on, honey, we'll have a good time."

"Oh, all right," I agreed without enthusiasm. What the hell was the difference.

I threw on a pair of jeans and a sweater and didn't even bother to put on any makeup. In half an hour, we were all rushing to Stan's car, parked on the street half a block away.

The jazz club was located in an all black neighborhood; in fact, Mae and Stan were the only white people in the place. Everybody knew them there and they got a friendly greeting; apparently Stan played sax there quite frequently. As we walked through the mellow, smoke-filled room to a table, I could tell that every male in the place was looking at me. I guess I really looked sexy, even the way I was dressed and with no makeup on.

After an hour of drinking beer and listening to the

music — which was very good — the musicians took a break and Stan joined us at the table, drink in hand. He played with the other musicians for no pay, just free drinks, apparently a common practice in L.A. jazz clubs.

Just as Stan sat down, the door opened, letting in a cold, damp gust of wind which we felt even though we were not sitting near the door. I looked up and there stood a flashily dressed black man in his late twenties, pipe in his mouth and full-length black cape draped over his shoulders as protection against the rain. He was the type of man whose presence is felt the moment he enters, and he seemed to take up the whole room. And he was staring straight at me. Instinctively I felt an unpleasant, cold chill, and it wasn't from the door being opened.

The man walked over to the bar and said something to the bartender. A moment later, he was making his way through the small, crowded room, drink in hand, toward our table.

Stan stood up to greet him. "Hey, Jimbo, what's happening, baby," he pumped the man's hand.

"Same as usual," the man replied, but didn't look at Stan; he just kept staring at me. "Say, Stan, my man, where have you been hiding *this?*"

He meant me, and I didn't like it. I never could stand people who talked about you as though you weren't there. I stared right back at him, a hard look on my face. But it seemed to turn him on even more.

"Gorgeous, ain't she? Hot stuff, that's what," said Stan. Hell, now he was doing it, I thought, talking about me as though I weren't there. "She's my . . ." and he winked; I couldn't believe it, but Mae and my mother laughed. ". . . tenant," he continued, breaking himself with laughter. "Jim Robinson, meet the sensational Miss Mary Clarissa Stevens."

"Ms.," I interrupted without smiling, "and soon to be *Mrs.*"

The others ignored it, but Jim Robinson's eyes took on a gleam, as though he had been challenged, it seemed to me. Well, whatever he thought, that wasn't what I was trying to do. What I was trying to do was to turn him off, which seemed to be an impossible task. There was something about the man that I just didn't like.

"And this is Mary Clarissa's mother, Mrs. Hattie Stevens," Stan was saying pleasantly.

"So pleased to meet you, Mrs. Stevens," said Jim Robinson graciously, finally looking away from me. But not for long; after a split second he was staring at me again. The man couldn't take his eyes off me.

Years ago, I would have physically tried to shrink away, but not now. I sat up even straighter in my chair, throwing my chest out, and stared back at him. Probably I would have been better off to shrink.

"I'm waiting . . ." Jim Robinson said to Stan.

We were all startled.

Robinson flashed an Ipana toothpaste smile. ". . . for you to invite me to join you."

"Hey, Jimbo, man, you got it," Stan replied, slapping him on the back and pulling over another chair for Robinson to be seated on.

Soon the musician's break was over, and Stan went back to play sax. As the evening progressed, I began to feel a strange attraction for Jim Robinson, even though my initial revulsion was still there.

We closed the place, not leaving until 2 a.m. On the way out, Jim took my arm, stopping me. His hand was strong and he had a firm touch, not at all unpleasant, I hated to admit to myself.

I just looked at him.

"I would like to see you again, Mary Clarissa," he said huskily.

So damned sure of himself, I thought. "No, thank you, Jim," I said flatly.

Still holding my arm, he reached into his pocket and in one lithe movement, flashed out a business card. "Just in case you change your mind," he said softly, then, his cape flapping in the wind, he was off into the dark, rainy night.

Did you ever see a Count Dracula movie? They always cast Jack Palance or Frank Langella or someone incredibly sexy like that, but who is sinister enough to scare the wits out of you even as he seduces you from the screen. And the women in the audience don't know whether they want to go to bed with him or drive a wooden stake through his heart, or both. Well, that was Jim Robinson in a nutshell, and it had nothing to do with his stupid black rain cape. It was a certain quality that exuded from him, a certain sense of power and sex appeal that grabbed and held you fast.

In the car on the way home, I tried not to think about Jim Robinson, focusing my mind on William, the man whom I loved and was going to marry. But it was impossible; Stan kept talking about his friend Jim.

"Now there's a guy who could help your show business career, Mary Clarissa," Stan was babbling on. "He's quite a dude."

"I don't have any show business career," I replied coldly. "And I'm getting married, remember?"

"Sure, sure," Stan said, and I saw him wink at my mother through the rear view mirror. What the hell was it, a conspiracy? I thought angrily.

Mae turned around in the front seat. "He sure is sexy, too," she added, smiling.

Fine, I thought, and she thinks I'm sexy, too. She'd probably like to have us both, maybe at the same time. What a kinky chick she was. I wanted no part of any of it, that was for sure.

"You know how he makes a living?" Stan continued. "By supplying plenty of the top brass at the studios and networks with you-know-what. That's how he could help your career, Mary Clarissa; he's got enough contacts to launch anyone, especially a doll who looks as good as you do."

"So he's a pusher," I mused. "I thought he was probably a pimp."

"Hush, Mary Clarissa," Mama said to me, as though I were a rude five-year-old, "Jim is a friend of Stan and Mae, and he seemed like . . ."

"I know, Mama," I interrupted in a bored tone, "he seemed like a 'nice young man.' Boy, Mama, your taste has certainly gone downhill. I never thought I'd hear you refer to a pusher as a 'nice young man.' "

"Well," said Mae, "at least he doesn't sell to kids."

"Big deal," was my answer to that.

I looked at his card, which I still held absentmindedly in my hand. It was on expensive paper, off white, with his name and phone number embossed in deep gold letters. I shoved it into my purse and forgot about it.

By the time we got back to the apartment, it was nearly three in the morning, but I rushed to the phone and dialed William's number.

After several rings, he answered the phone in a sleepy voice.

"Hi," I whispered. "I missed you. I just had to call."

"Hey, babe, I'm glad you did," he said with sleepy enthusiasm, trying to come fully awake.

I held the phone close to my face, wishing I were there in his apartment with him, in bed.

"I tried to call you at about 11," he was saying, "then again at 11:30, then at midnight . . ." He sounded a bit perturbed.

"Oh, wow," I said. "I let Mama talk me into going out with her and our neighbors. We went to this funky little jazz club out on Western."

"Was it good?" he asked, believing me, relieved.

"So-so," I said. "Jazz was pretty good." I stayed on the

phone with him for half an hour, not wanting to hang up, telling him all the trivial details of the evening. I left Jim Robinson completely out of the story, as though he didn't exist. Then we hung up and I went straight to bed, wishing I were with William.

But during the night, I had a dream about Jim Robinson. In the morning, I couldn't remember exactly what the dream was about, but it haunted me all day long, casting a cloud over an otherwise fun day with William.

As usual, he noticed something was bothering me. He was such a good, sensitive man, and I really loved him, as he loved me.

"It's only this stupid cold that's bothering me," I said. "Don't let it spoil your day." I squeezed his hand affectionately.

But he could always tell when I was lying, and he could now. However, he said nothing more about it, and as the day progressed, I began to snap out of my strange mood. That night, I went home with him and, after a light midnight snack of cheese, crackers, and white wine, we went to bed and made love. As usual, it was satisfying and wonderful.

The months went by happily, and soon it was time to select the date for our wedding. Jim Robinson was the farthest thing from my mind; I had succeeded in blocking out all feelings and thoughts of that evening at the jazz club.

I went out shopping for a wedding dress and wound up selecting one at Lerner's, an inexpensive shop on Hollywood Boulevard, next door to the more expensive Broadway Department Store, which I couldn't afford. On the hanger, it was a plain, simple white shirtwaist dress, street length, but when I tried it on, all the other women in the fitting room looked at me admiringly, some jealously. That, I never minded. The old competitive streak coming out again, I guess. I went to a fabric store on Fairfax Avenue and bought a small remnant of white netting out of which I made a simple, short veil. The day before my wedding, I would clip some flowers from a garden on the block and attach them to the veil. Anything to save a little money. Stan and Mae would stand up for us in the small non-denominational chapel where our wedding ceremony was to take place. Afterward, Mama said she'd take us all out to dinner at the inexpensive French restaurant she was so proud of having found.

It was such a happy time for me. I would walk along Hollywood Boulevard, then turn onto Vine Street, reading the names of actors and actresses who had their stars embossed on the shiny tile sidewalk. Sure, they were all big stars in movies and television, but were they as happy as me? No way, I thought, no one could be as happy as I was. I had everything I wanted, and that was more than most people could say, even movie stars, from what I knew about them.

What I didn't know was that fate was about to step in, as it sometimes does, and change my life completely.

CHAPTER 9

Most of the time in L.A., the smog hangs over the sprawling city like a shroud, making it difficult for people with any kind of respiratory problem to breathe, and marring the natural beauty of the city that really isn't a city but a collection of pretty, neatly landscaped suburbs. Old-timers talk about the days before the coming of the factories and the countless automobiles which pollute the air with their foul waste products. Occasionally, though, a strong wind blows over Los Angeles and, like a God-sent janitor, cleans up the upstairs of the city, sweeping the filthy, choking smog away. For the next day or so, the skies are brilliant blue and the air smells, even feels, fresh and clean.

That was how the day started out on that fateful Tuesday, a day which I will never forget no matter how long I am fortunate enough to live. It started out so nicely, with my mother and I up early, sipping coffee at our small fold-away table which she had covered with a pretty flowered tablecloth. We had just finished a light breakfast of orange juice and whole wheat toast with real butter spread on it, and we were relaxing over our coffee, watching assorted birds lighting on the tree outside our window. The curtains were pulled wide open, allowing the rays of soft morning sun to brighten the clean but shabby room. I had been spending as much time as I could with Mama lately, realizing that after William and I were married, I wouldn't be seeing her as often. Even though Mama and I didn't always agree, she was really a very good mother to me, and always had been.

"Well," I commented, "everything's all set. The wedding's only eleven days and one hour away."

My mother's eyes had a faraway look. "That's what I did just before your father and I got married," she said sadly. "I counted the days and the hours, even the minutes."

I started to change the subject, but she continued.

"What do you think being married is like, Mary Clarissa? Well, it doesn't matter what you think, honey. You have no way of knowing until you go through it."

I didn't like the way the conversation was going, and I particularly didn't like the intense tone that was beginning to creep into my mother's voice.

"Mama . . ."

"Hush," she interrupted, smiling, "let your old mother talk for a while, won't you?"

"Okay, Mama, but . . ."

"You're really going through with it, aren't you, Mary Clarissa?" she said.

"Of course, Mama," I replied, looking away, trying to tune her out.

"So my little girl is all grown up, and wants to live her own life. Well, I don't blame you, honey." She smiled wistfully. "But I won't be seeing you so much anymore. And my grownup little girl will never be a big star, rich and famous . . ."

"Mama, I have every right to make my own decisions and live my own life . . ." I was becoming very agitated.

"Of course, you do, honey." She reached over and touched my hand. "And I want you to know that I accept everything you are doing and planning and . . ." Suddenly she put her hands over her face and burst out crying, huge sobs that tore through her body like convulsions.

My head was beginning to throb from the tension. I got up, walked around the table and put my arms around her.

"Mama," I begged, "please stop. Please try to control yourself. I'm happy and I want you to be happy."

"Oh, honey," she cried, "all I ever wanted was for you to be happy, to be somebody, to be somebody important! You were my hope, my only hope . . ."

I walked away from her and began pacing around the small room. Memories of my childhood began to seep into my mind, memories of not having any friends, of not fitting in at school, of my body being violated by a gang of low-lifes who thought they were human beings, of being helpless in the ugly, steamy ghetto, of the feeling that the bottom was dropping out of my world whenever my parents fought.

I turned on my mother and shrieked at her. "But I am somebody — I am! I am somebody!" I shouted over and over, then I too burst into tears. I ran over and knelt down beside her. "Aren't I, Mama? Aren't I somebody? You always said I was," I whimpered, "you always said I was special . . ."

She was beginning to calm down. "Of course you are, honey," she said soothingly, stroking my hair. "You're very special and you always will be."

Now I felt that I had to get out of there, take a walk, anything. The room seemed to be getting smaller and I was having trouble breathing. I just couldn't seem to get enough air into my lungs.

My mother got up and went to wash her face, then she came out of the bathroom and sat down at the table again.

"Mama," I said, "I'm going out for a walk. Why don't you come with me?"

"No," she said, "I'm all right now. You go ahead and

take your walk. I'm going to shower and wash my hair, then I'll straighten up around here. Maybe when you come back, we can go out and have a nice lunch at the Sizzler's." She smiled. "It'll be my treat."

"Well, if you're sure you're okay."

"Yes, I am," she assured me. "Now you go ahead. I know how you like to walk, and it looks like a beautiful day out."

I picked up my purse and opened the door, and she called out, "Mary Clarissa, I'm awfully sorry for that outburst. I really didn't mean to upset you. I don't know what comes over me sometimes."

"It's okay, Mama," I said. "Just forget about it." I walked over to her and kissed her on the cheek. I'll be back in a little while, and later we'll go to the Sizzler's. Okay?"

"Have a nice walk," she smiled.

I left the apartment and felt better as soon as I was out of there. It really was a beautiful morning, and I walked along briskly until I got to Hollywood Boulevard, then I began to stroll along, people-watching and window shopping. I studied the hippies, wondering what made them live the way they did and if they would ever rejoin society. They were all over the boulevard, scrounging for change, making a point of their self-imposed poverty and disdain for the mainstream. Then I noticed a woman who looked about 65 but was probably only 40. She was a hunch-back, and she was filthy, walking along the street with a vacant look on her face. Had she chosen to drop out, or had circumstances beaten her down, befouling her life? I realized that at one time she must have been young like me, full of hope, full of feelings and caring about what went on around her. Now she was a zombie, wandering in the streets of glamorous Hollywood, just barely managing to exist.

I shook my mind free of these negative, depressing thoughts. None of these people had anything to do with me. I had my whole life ahead of me, I had made my decisions as to what course to take, and I was determined to be happy on this beautiful morning. And I made it a point not to look at those stars on the shiny sidewalk, the stars with the names embossed in the middle of them. That had nothing to do with me either.

I walked around for about an hour, and on the way home I stopped at a thrift store and bought my mother a corsage with a fake flower and a pretty red ribbon. She could wear it when we went out to lunch, it would make it like a kind of celebration. Mama liked things like that, and I really wanted her to be happy.

Those were my thoughts as I rounded the corner of our block and saw the ambulance double-parked in front of our building. It was a Fire Department Paramedic unit and I was not at all alarmed; ambulances were a familiar sight, what with elderly people having coronaries and young people O.D.'ing on drugs. But when I approached the building and saw Stan coming out of the walkway to our apartment, a stricken expression on his blood-drained face, I was instantly frightened. I quickened my pace and began to run toward him. As I passed the doorway to Stan's apartment, I saw that it was open and Mae was leaning against it, sobbing.

Stan rushed forward and grabbed me. "Honey, don't go in there. Let me tell you what happened."

"Mama!" I screamed, tearing away from him, almost knocking him down on the sidewalk. "Oh, my God!"

I ran up our walkway; the door to our apartment was wide open. "What are they doing?" I screamed hysterically. Somehow, in my panic, I became furious that our door was open like that. It seemed like an invasion of our privacy. "What the hell are they doing, Goddammit!" I screamed and shouted every profanity I could think of.

I rushed into the apartment. There were two paramedics in the bathroom; one was bending over something; the other was at the bathroom door. When he saw me, he stepped forward.

"You can't go in there now, miss," he said, blocking my way.

I shoved at him, trying to kick him, but apparently he was well-trained for situations like this. He restrained me, and as much as I wanted to, he would not let me go into that room.

"Do you live here, miss?" the paramedic asked quietly, when I had stopped struggling.

"Yes," I told him, "with my mother. Now please tell me, what the hell is going on?! What's happened?"

"Are you Miss Stevens?" he asked. I guess Stan had given him all the information.

Suddenly I turned and ran into the bathroom, and what I saw in there is impossible for me to deal with, even to this day. My mother was lying on the bathroom floor in a pool of blood, unconscious, her eyes closed tightly. The paramedic bending over her was cleaning the blood off her face, or whatever he was doing. There was blood everywhere. For years afterward, I would gag at the sight of catsup, remembering this grim, sickening scene.

Now I just stood there, frozen in my tracks, my mouth wide open as if to scream, but no sound would come out. The last thing I remember seeing was the startled look on the kneeling paramedic's face as he looked over his shoulder and saw me standing there. Then I fainted.

When I opened my eyes, I was lying in a hospital bed. The smell of antiseptic, which I have always hated, burned in my nostrils. I moved my eyes to the right and saw William's profile; he was sitting in a chair beside the bed. On the chair across from the bed was a woman's purse, which I recognized as belonging to Mae. For a merciful thirty seconds or so, I could not remember what had happened, and I wondered what I was doing there. Then it all came back in a rush, tearing through my mind and my insides.

William, seeing that I had regained consciousness, stood up quickly and walked to the bed. He sat down on the edge and took my hand. I could see tears in his eyes; I had never seen him cry before.

"Mama?" I asked him, already knowing the answer.

"She's gone," he whisperred, choking on the words. "They tried to save her, but she died about fifteen minutes ago."

I was numb. I couldn't feel anything, nothing at all. And I didn't want to.

"What happened?" I asked calmly.

"She must have slipped in the bathtub and hit her head on the tub."

"Yes," I said evenly. "I remember, she didn't have any clothes on. The paramedic was working on her, and she didn't have any clothes on. She had said she was going to take a shower." I had absolutely no feelings whatsoever.

"Mae said she was watering the lawn when she heard a scream coming from your apartment," William went on, his voice trembling. "She ran back to her apartment to get the pass key. When she got in there, she found your mother unconscious and she called the paramedics. They got there almost immediately, she said."

"Yes, I know," I said. "I've heard they're very good, very efficient. I'm sure everyone tried their best to save her."

William, realizing I was in deep shock, sat there on the edge of the bed, holding my hand, talking to me. I have no idea to this day what he talked about; I had tuned him out.

The wedding, of course, had to be postponed. Mae probably handled the details, I don't know, because for the next six weeks I walked around in a total fog, completely detached from the world around me. My memories of that period are very vague, but I remember William being around, comforting me, supporting me. What a patient, caring person he is. He really loved me so much.

When I started coming out of it, I found myself in William's apartment, where I had been staying. One afternoon I started to feel more alert, more aware of my surroundings, like the fog that had been all around me was finally lifting.

When William came home from work that evening, he noticed the change immediately, and he smiled with relief and took me in his arms.

"Looks like you're finally getting to be yourself again," he said happily.

"Yes," I agreed, but deep down I knew I wasn't myself, and I wondered if I ever would be again. It was me on the outside, I could tell by William's reaction. But inside, I had changed.

The next night I told William that I wanted to go home.

"Back to the apartment?" he frowned. "Do you think it's wise? I mean, are you ready for that?"

"I'm ready," I said.

"Okay," he agreed, but hesitantly. "When?"

"How about right now," I told him.

"Come on, honey, wait until morning. I'll drive you there before I go to work."

"Fine," I agreed.

He made love to me that night, and I went through the motions mechanically, like a robot. It was pleasant, and I enjoyed it, but unemotionally, lovelessly.

William drove me back to the apartment early the next morning.

"Do you want me to come in with you?" he asked.

"No," I replied, "I'm fine."

"Okay," he agreed reluctantly. "But I'll come over right after work."

"You don't have to check on me," I said flatly. "I said I'd be okay; don't you trust me? I'm not a mental case, you know."

"Of course I do, honey." He kissed me and drove off to work.

I took the keys out of my purse, opened the door and walked in. It was as though nothing had happened. The apartment was spotless; Mae must have been going in and cleaning it at least twice a week.

I spent the day just sitting on the daybed, listening to the radio absentmindedly, but on one level, the beginning of a plan was formulating in my mind.

William called at about 6:30.

"Feel like going out for something to eat?" he asked, trying to sound casual. "I can pick you up in about an hour and we can grab a bite somewhere, maybe go to a movie afterward."

"No," I told him, "I think I'll stay home tonight."

"Whatever you say," he replied. "I'll call you later on, okay?"

"Sure," I said briskly.

"I love you very much," he said into the phone, and hung up. He was patient and understanding, but I could tell he was worried about me, about our relationship. It didn't bother me in the least; in fact, nothing seemed to bother me now.

I looked at the 5 x 7 enlargement of a snapshot of Mama and me that sat on the end table in a white plastic frame. To me, it wasn't as if Mama was dead, it was as if she had just gone on a trip and would be back in a couple of days. The death of a loved one is one of the hardest things to accept, and although I didn't realize it then, I just wasn't accepting it. This was another factor that would soon change my life.

CHAPTER 10

"Hi," I said into the phone, using my most professional, yet sensual voice. "This is Mary Clarissa Stevens." I looked at the fancy white business card with the gold embossed letters.

There was a moment of silence on the other end of the phone.

"Well, I'll be!" Jim Robinson finally said. "You gorgeous creature! Have you been out of town?" He certainly was conceited, assuming that because I had not yet called him, I must have been "out of town." But now I really didn't care about his character, or lack of it.

"You might say that," I answered, delighted that he remembered me.

In the two weeks that I had been back in the apartment where I had lived with my mother all those years, a new Mary Clarissa Stevens had emerged. We all have different sides to our personalities; which route we take is a matter of choice, and sometimes we don't have conscious control. Now I wanted a successful career as an actress, I wanted fame and money, I wanted to be somebody — all the things my mother had always wanted for me. And I simply didn't care whether or not I ever became Mrs. William Jones; it just didn't matter to me anymore. Maybe it was a psychological attempt to keep my mother alive; maybe it was guilt at having disappointed her; I don't know. But this was what had happened to me, and I was quite happy with my new attitude, and comfortable with it.

"So how've you been, sexy lady?" Jim Robinson was breathing into the phone. Before I could answer, he said, "Say, look, let's not talk on the phone. I want to see you. How about I pick you up at around nine? Give me the address again." He didn't even wait for an answer as to whether I wanted to go out with him. Of course, since I had called him, it was logical for him to assume that that was why I had called him. But he sure didn't give me a chance to say no, either.

I gave him the address, not again, because I had never given it to him before. He was a smooth mover, good-looking and sexy, and more important, he could help my career. What did I have to lose?

I had a few hours to get ready, so I treated myself to a warm, scented bubble bath, then went through my closet trying to decide what to wear. I dressed to look classy. Sexy, I looked anyway; I didn't have to try.

Jim Robinson drove a Mercedes, an older model; he picked me up and we went to an intimate little restaurant on La Cienega for a late dinner. He seemed to know everyone there, and he was proud to introduce me to them. We sat at a candlelit table and made small talk; mostly I remember him constantly complimenting me on my face and figure, with nicely-phrased words and smouldering looks. When I told him about my mother, he was appropriately sympathetic.

The evening was very pleasant and I enjoyed it, but I wasn't out for a good time. I wanted Jim Robinson to help me with my career, and I was willing to pay any price for it. I planned to play the situation by ear.

Finally, on the way home, Jim said, "So how's your career going?"

I didn't know how much Stan had told him about me and my almost non-existent acting career, so I decided to bluff.

"Well," I began nonchalantly, "I've been on a little self-imposed hiatus since my mother died. It was something I really needed, to get my head on straight again. But now I'm back in the running, so there shouldn't be any problems."

"Great," he said. "I'm sure there won't be any problems for a chick like you." He looked into my eyes and smiled slightly. "In fact, I'll guarantee it."

I could tell by his tone of voice that it was obvious to him what I was up to. It made me feel a little queasy at first, but I put the feeling out of my mind. I was achieving my purpose; this was the first step.

I was surprised when he drove straight to my apartment and pulled the Mercedes over to the curb. No pass?

I was debating whether to ask him in for a nightcap. All I had was a half-empty bottle of some cheap wine; I was new at this game. The decision was made for me.

"May I call you?" he asked, every bit the gentleman. "I'd like to see you again."

I paused, not wanting to seem too anxious, even though I realized he already knew the answer. "Well, yes," I said evenly but seductively, "that would be very nice."

He whipped out a gold pen and one of his fancy cards. "Here," he offered, "write down your phone number on this."

I wrote down my phone number, having enough sense not to put my name next to it. Let him write it down as soon as I went inside, I figured. This guy probably had plenty of girl friends.

Suddenly he took my face in both hands, drew me close and kissed me, passionately, forcing my mouth open with his tongue. It took me by surprise and instantly I felt a surge of passion charging through my body. I melted, wanting to make it with him right there in the car. Then he gently pushed me away, rubbing his hand lightly over my breasts. The nipples were hard and firm, and he looked into my eyes, smiling slightly.

"You'd better get inside now, Mary Clarissa," he said. "I'd walk you to your door, but I'm parked in the red. Hate to get a ticket and pay out hard-earned money to The Man." He started the engine. What a bastard.

I opened the car door and got out. As I did, I stuck out my ass and moved it from side to side, slowly and seductively. He didn't seem to, but I was pretty damned sure he noticed.

"Goodnight, Jim," I breathed over my shoulder, then went inside the apartment. I tossed my purse on a chair and began to get ready for bed. I have to admit that I was sorry that I was going to bed alone, but I was happy that I felt I had taken the first big step toward launching my career. When I couldn't fall asleep I thought of calling William, but didn't. Somehow, he didn't excite me anymore. Believe it or not, the thought that I was using people to my own advantage, without giving a care in the world for them, didn't even occur to me. I suppose that's what ambition can do to you if you're not careful.

CHAPTER 11

On my second date with Jim Robinson, I went to bed with him. He was a marvelous lover, skilled, with an incredible knack for bringing a girl to the heights of ecstasy. On the third date, I became hooked on him, sexually, and on the fourth, I packed a few things and moved in with him, at his request.

"Think what a good time we'll have," he breathed in my ear, "every morning, every night, all night long, if you so desire."

I called William and lied to him, not caring whether he believed me or not.

"Hon," I said into the phone, "I need a little vacation. I'm going to take a couple of months and go to the mountains or somewhere."

There was a pause. "But where are you going exactly?" he asked.

"I don't know," I told him. "I'll figure it out later. But I've got to get out of this town."

"Can I see you before you leave?" he asked, his voice trembling. I hadn't seen him in weeks and he really missed me.

"No," I said, "there won't be time. I'm leaving right away."

"Call me when you get back, please, Mary Clarissa," he

said, sounding like he was about to cry. "I love you very much."

"Goodbye, William," I said, and hung up the phone.

I shudder when I think of how hard-hearted I had become, without even realizing it.

At Jim Robinson's, the lifestyle was completely different from anything I'd ever experienced. There were all-night parties with plenty of wine and marijuana, which I tried once and couldn't stand. Jim laughed at this and seemed pleased.

His friends were many and varied. Most of them, I think, were girls whom he had had affairs with, ranging from young, long-haired hippies who wore headbands and Indian clothes, to middle-class looking housewifetypes who had probably never had any man so good in bed. And all these girls seemed to be jealous of me, Jim's latest chick. That, I really got off on! He didn't have as many male friends, but there were a few rough types whom I wasn't too crazy about, and one guy whom I'd swear had "eyes" for Jim. He probably did.

Jim lived in an old, high-ceilinged duplex in Culver City, not too far from one of the major studios. There were Oriental carpets on the floors of two of the rooms (I found out later they were imitations) and in his bedroom he installed mirror tiles on the ceiling. The bed on which we made love and slept was huge, with big, soft pillows and red satin sheets.

Two weeks went by, and I realized that Jim had said nothing about my career, other than to ask me in a sarcastic tone why my agent wasn't sending me out more. Basically, I guess, I'm an honest person; I yearned to lay my cards on the table and ask him to use some of his influence to get me an interview, anything. But my instincts told me this would be the wrong approach. He knew damn well what I wanted, and he would help me, whenever he got tired of playing his cruel little game.

Almost every day, he would go out for a few hours, "on business," as he put it, and one day when he came home he said he wanted to talk to me.

"Mary Clarissa," he began, "it's really bothering me to see a gorgeous, talented chick like you not working. Now I realize that it's not your fault at all; it's just that — and I don't want you to get insulted — you don't have a very good agent."

No kidding, I thought, saying nothing. He just loved to play cat and mouse.

"Mary Clarissa," he continued, "would you consider changing agents?"

"Of course," I said, "I would change to a better agent."

"Well," he said, "it just so happens that I am acquainted with a fairly good agent, whom I'm sure would love to meet you. If you make your usual good impression, he'll probably sign you."

"Fine," I said, "I'd like to meet him."

A few days later, I sat in the reception room of the plush offices of Robert Todd. Inside, I was boiling over with excitement; outside, I presented my practiced poise and warm friendliness. In back of my mind, I wondered what I should do if the agent tried to make me.

As I should have realized, the problem never came up. Jim had sent me, and the agent was probably one of Jim's "client's" for drugs.

Robert Todd seemed delighted to meet me, and I could see he was impressed. I don't know how many other aspiring young actresses Jim had sent him, but he treated me like someone very special.

He looked through my leather bound portfolio. One of Jim's friends had come over a few days before and photographed me, rushing the processing through so I would have the new pictures in time for this interview. They had turned out quite good.

"Mary Clarissa," the agent was saying, "not only are

you a very beautiful girl, but you photograph even better, if that's possible."

"Thank you, Mr. Todd," I said, beaming.

He chit-chatted with me for fifteen minutes, then gave me something to read. When I saw the scene, I was very relieved. It was one I already knew, having performed it in acting class. I didn't tell that to the agent, though; I just pretended to read the scene. He seemed quite impressed.

"Excellent, Mary Clarissa," Todd said sincerely. "You're a very good cold reader." He smiled. "A beautiful girl who can also act!"

"Well, I love acting," I told him. "It's my whole life." I knew it was what he wanted to hear.

Soon the conversation got around to the subject of my signing with him.

"I'm very complimented," I told Robert Todd. "Just give me a couple of days, and I'll call you and we can set up another appointment and we can take it from there." It was what Jim had told me to say.

I left the agent's office, and instead of phoning for a taxi as Jim had instructed, I decided to walk for a while. I was full of energy and enthusiasm; I had the feeling that Robert Todd could get me parts, and that this was only the beginning. I walked over to Sunset and Doheny, then across town to Wilshire, a good couple of miles. Now I was in Beverly Hills, and I strolled along Wilshire, looking in the windows of expensive department stores — I. Magnin, Saks, all of them. I could imagine myself a star, shopping in these fancy stores, buying anything and everything I wanted. The really exclusive shops are on Rodeo in Beverly Hills, but to me, Wilshire Boulevard was heaven. I was used to Lerner's on Hollywood Boulevard.

Finally I decided I'd better call Jim.

"Where the hell have you been!" he yelled into the phone. "I thought I told you to get in a taxi and come right home after the interview. Don't tell me you lost the money I gave you . . !"

"Of course not, Jim," I said sweetly. "I decided to take a walk and do some window shopping. And have I got good news for you . . ."

"I already know the news," he said. "Now get in a cab and get the hell home! Dumb broad," I heard him mutter as he hung up the phone.

When I got back to Jim's apartment, he was waiting for me at the door.

"You idiot!" he shouted, slapping me across the face, hard. "Don't you ever pull anything like that again! From now on, I'm your personal manager, and you do just what I tell you. Got that!?"

I was stunned. I turned around and strode into the bedroom, got out my old suitcase and began to pack. There was no way I was going to put up with anything like that.

"I don't need this bastard," I muttered to myself. "I'll find someone else to help with my career."

I walked out into the living room, carrying my packed suitcase, and didn't even look at Jim, sitting on the sofa.

He jumped up and stepped in front of the door. "Please, babe," he said quietly. "I'm sorry. I just lost my temper. I don't want you to leave." He took the suitcase from my hand. "Come, sit and talk with me. Tell me about your interview."

"I thought you already knew all about it," I said coldly.

He took me in his arms. "Todd just loved you," he said, "and he'll get you work. When you didn't come home, I got real worried, that's all; that's why I blew up. Really, babe, I'm so proud of you . . ."

He really seemed sincere in his apology. I decided to stay, at least for a while.

He said, "You know, Mary Clarissa, I'm really getting stuck on you, and I didn't think I would. Most of those girls that come over when we have our little parties and gatherings, I used to screw every one of them."

Well, that had been obvious.

"But since you're here, they don't seem all that great anymore. When I asked you to move in here, I figured I could have you here any time I wanted you, and them as well, on occasion, anyway. I've never been a one-woman man; that's not my style."

For the first time, he didn't seem to be game-playing. He sounded sincere and I began to listen attentively. This was another side to Jim Robinson.

"And you're not the first aspiring actress I've sent to Todd. He was so enthusiastic about you, almost like you cast some kind of spell over him." He laughed. "You're not a witch, are you?"

I put my arms around him. "If I am, I'm a good witch," I teased.

He held me at arm's length and looked at me. "On the phone, Todd kept going on about how you have star quality. Well, it doesn't only apply to your professional life. You have star quality as a person also. I want you to be my star, Mary Clarissa. Will you marry me?"

I was astounded. I never expected a proposal from a guy like Jim Robinson.

"You look like you're in shock," he smiled. "I'm really not such a bad dude, you know. That's just an act I put on. When you grow up in the streets, you learn to do that early on. But with you, Mary Clarissa, I don't feel a need to do anything like that. With you I feel I can be myself."

I wondered if he was being himself when he had hit me just before. Which was worse, his act or his real self?

"So what do you say? We can drive to Vegas, say, day after tomorrow, get married, do a little gambling, take in a few shows . . ."

"Jim," I told him, "you've got to give me some time." I winced as thoughts of William and the real love we had shared flashed through my mind. I tried to steady myself by focusing on my aim in life, my career.

"Okay," he flashed a smile. "Just let me know that you'll marry me by, say, noon tomorrow."

Now what was I going to do? I didn't love Jim and I didn't want to love William. And I didn't want to get married at all. All I wanted now was to have a successful career, the way my mother had always wanted me to.

The next day, I walked into the bedroom and found Jim going through my closet, packing a few of my things into a suitcase. By the door was his suitcase, already packed.

A flash of anger came over me. "Jim," I said, "what the hell are you doing with my things?"

He looked up, honestly surprised. "Just putting together some things you'll need in Vegas. I figure we can stay a few days, kind of a honeymoon."

I walked over and took the suitcase away from him. "Jim," I said, "you don't know me very well. I haven't consented, first of all, and second of all, I am quite capable of packing my own suitcase — *if* we are going somewhere together."

I thought he would get angry, but he didn't. His eyes took on an expression of challenge, similar to the way he had looked that first night I met him at the jazz club on Western.

"Very well," he said calmly. "We don't have to get married right now. I just thought that marriage was what you wanted. After all, weren't you going to marry some dude just recently?"

"But I didn't, did I?!" My eyes flashed with triumph. "I'm a pretty independent chick, you see."

Somehow, this turned him on. Without another word, he pushed me down on the bed and made love to me, forcefully, lustfully, and I loved every minute of it.

When it was over, we lay there exhausted. After an

hour, there as a light knock on the door.

Jim looked at his watch. "Oh, hell, I forgot all about Tommy." He got up and quickly dressed. "You stay in here, doll," he said, and went to answer the door.

Why should I, I thought, getting up and dressing. I went into the living room and found Jim talking quietly to a man who looked like he belonged in the zoo, in the gorilla cage. As I came into the room, Jim was handing him some money. I walked by them, pretending not to notice, and went into the kitchen and poured myself a glass of 7-Up.

Soon I heard the door slam, and Jim came into the kitchen. He got a bottle of scotch out of the cabinet and fixed himself a double.

"What the hell was that?" I asked, referring to the gorilla. "He must be 7 feet tall and 4 feet wide. Friend of yours?"

Jim chuckled. "That's Tommy," he said. "A business associate and more valuable to me than any friend."

I had no desire to know what that meant, so I didn't pursue it. Eventually, though, I was to find out, but that's another story.

A few days later, Jim and I went to Robert Todd's office to work out a deal whereby I would be Todd's client. Jim handled the negotiations. Mostly I just listened, asking an occasional question.

When we left the agent's office, I had a contract and a new name as well. Todd had thought that Mary Clarissa Stevens was too long a name, too hard for people to remember.

"Claire Stevens," Todd said. "Now doesn't that sound great? That's a star name." He beamed.

It sounded good to me too, but I looked at Jim for approval. If he was going to be my personal manager, he would make the decisions, at least when other people were present.

"Well, I don't know," Jim said slowly, playing the game. "I'll have to give it some thought."

"Fine," said Todd, and he instructed the secretary to leave blank the space on the contract for "professional name."

After we left Todd's office, Jim and I went to a Hamburger Hamlet for lunch.

"Well, Claire," he said, smiling, "we got a lot accomplished this morning, didn't we?"

"You bet," I agreed, "and I hope he comes up with something soon."

"He will," Jim said confidently. "He's not a real heavyweight agent, but he'll do for now, until more important industry people start getting to know you and take an interest."

It sounded terrific to me.

"At first, he'll probably be able to get you walk-ons, bit parts, get your feet wet. But your star is going to rise, babe, I got a feeling."

I had the same feeling, and I didn't have to wait long for my first professional acting part. It was on a TV show, a cop series. I was to play the part of a tenant in a high-rise building who is sitting around the pool in a bikini when a murder takes place in the building. The police are questioning everybody in the building and my big line is: "Gee, officer, I wish I could help you, but I didn't see or hear a thing." Then I was supposed to jump into the pool.

The night before the filming, I couldn't sleep. I kept going over and over my line, saying it every which way, rehearsing in front of Jim's long, gold-framed mirror. I practiced and rehearsed, and Jim was amused by my antics, but I could tell he was also proud of me.

"Babe," he said, "I appreciate that you want to do a good job, but I do think you're overdoing it. I mean, don't get yourself so uptight that you flub your lines.

"You mean 'line,' " I laughed nervously. "One line!

And yet I'm more worried about this one dumb line than I've ever been about anything in my whole life, I think!"

"Well, that makes sense," he said. "It's your first job and it's very important to you. But I'm sure you'll do great. Anyway, anything is forgiven when a girl looks like you. The director'll probably flip out when you sashay out onto that set."

I detected a note of jealousy in his voice. Too bad for him, I thought, he would just have to get used to it. I had no plans to go to bed with any director, anyhow. If I had any intention of having affairs with every guy who thought I was sexy, I'd go into a different business and make plenty of money at it: prostitution. But that, of course, wasn't my thing.

My call was for 11:00 a.m. on location at a building near Sunset and Doheny, where they had a huge, beautiful swimming pool on the roof. I was there two hours early, checked in with the assistant director, then made myself unobtrusive until I was called for wardrobe, which is usually done the day before, but not always if they're running behind schedule. They had wardrobe set up in a vacant apartment, also makeup.

"Wow," the wardrobe mistress said as I walked into apartment 1102, "I've got two bikinis for you to try on, and you're going to look sensational in either one."

My costume wound up being a light lavender, low cut bikini, which contrasted beautifully with my dark skin, and showed my figure to its very best advantage.

At the pool, the director had me and the two actors playing cops run through the scene with the camera crew. Afterward, he came over to me.

"Claire," he said, "you're doing great."

"Thank you," I replied, much relieved.

"Now I think we're going to be able to get a few good closeups of you, though you look so good in that bikini that I'm tempted to keep the shots mostly medium and long."

"Oh," I said, not knowing what to answer. When I saw him smile, I smiled back.

"So," he went on, "after you tell the officer that you didn't see or hear a thing, smile the way you did just now and say, 'Maybe I was just under water.' Then, turn, the camera will be pulling back out of closeup then, and jump into the pool. Got that?"

"Of course," I said confidently.

He called a late lunch break then, and instead of eating I went over and over my new instructions. I really wanted to do a good job with my "big scene."

We did the scene six times, and I was beginning to worry that I was doing something wrong. Luckily, after it was all done, the director came over to me again.

"Claire," he said happily, "you were terrific."

"Thank you," I said, confused. Why had they needed so many takes?

"You did everything right in each and every take," he continued. "You're just a natural."

I suppose he realized how inexperienced I was. You couldn't fool a pro, I guessed.

"I really shouldn't have taken so much time with that little scene," he said, "but I've always felt that each and every part is important to a show, even the bits. I had you filmed from just about every angle; we'll use the best."

"Good," I said.

He looked at his watch. "I won't need you anymore today, so you can go now." He smiled. "We'll work together again, I hope, and soon."

Later I would find out that it was very unusual for TV directors to take so much time and trouble with a relatively unimportant scene like mine. Other directors, ones who didn't believe in taking time with small scenes, would do the same, because of me being in the scene. But now, I wondered whether the director had been saying what he really meant or just flattering me. Plenty of insincerity went on in Hollywood; that much I had already learned.

The next day the agent called Jim. I saw a big smile come over Jim's face as he listened to what the agent had to say. After he hung up, he picked me up and whirled around the room with me.

"You made a terrific splash!" he went on and on excitedly. "Oh, baby, you're going to be a star, just mark my words. I knew it, I knew it, I knew it the minute I laid eyes on you!"

I was delighted. Now I couldn't wait for my next job.

I didn't have to wait long. Two weeks later, I was on the set at Universal Studios with a part in a situation comedy. This time I had four lines, and one of them was very funny.

"I hope I can deliver the line and make people laugh," I had said to Jim the night before.

"It doesn't have to be funny," he told me. "They put in a laugh track anyway. All you have to do is look good, and you sure don't have any trouble with that."

The sit-com director seemed to be very impressed with me, too. I got along well with the other actors, the crew, even the extras. Working in front of the camera was really getting to be fun.

For the next six months or so, I worked a lot, getting all kinds of small roles in just about every TV series and several movies. On one movie of the week, the director liked me so much that he expanded my scene, adding a little dialogue and lots of action.

"You're very charismatic, Claire," he told me, putting his arm around my shoulder. "And that's what the viewers want. Most of them don't know good acting from bad, anyway."

I hoped he didn't mean that I was a bad actress. But he probably did.

"Now see that young lady over there?" He pointed to a young, kind of pretty but plain character actress sitting off to the side working on her lines. "She happens to be a very fine, talented actress. She can carry any scene, and she's done a lot of excellent work on stage. But she'll never be a movie or TV star. She just doesn't have that extra spark, that extra something that makes the audience feel like they know her and would want her to be their friend. You know what I mean?" he asked.

I nodded.

"Well, you do have that quality. Star quality, it's called. You don't have to be a great actress, that's unimportant."

It got to the point where the various directors were asking for me, and always happy to see me when I reported for work on the set. Todd, the agent, was able to get me more money with each part, and better billing. I loved seeing my name on the credits: Claire Stevens, in big letters or small letters, it looked terrific to me. If only my mother could be here to see it, I would think, and tears of sorrow and guilt would start. She had passed away without any hope of her dream being fulfilled.

And I wondered whether William ever saw me on the screen, whether he still loved me. As far as I knew, he had made no attempt to contact me. Of course, how could I blame him? Did I still have feelings for him? I honestly don't know. At this point, I don't think I loved anyone. All my energy was devoted to furthering my career; love was the farthest thing from my mind.

CHAPTER 12

One day I picked up the phone and was greeted by a very happy agent.

"Claire," Todd said excitedly, "wait'll you hear this. No, no, no," he stopped himself, "I'd better talk to Jim first."

"Jim's not home," I said. "Shall I have him call you when he gets in?" I was dying to know what he had to say, but I wasn't about to let him know that. Besides, I figured, he can't wait to tell someone; he'll probably tell me anyway.

Sure enough. "Oh, the hell with it," he said. "This is what's happening. Carolyn Barr wants to meet you. And for the second lead on a new sit-com!"

My heart raced, but I spoke calmly. "Fantastic," I said. "Tell me something about the part. Then you can talk to Jim about when to set up the appointment."

"Honey," he said with exasperation. "I said *Carolyn Barr*. She's one of *the* top casting directors, in case you hadn't heard!"

Of course I knew that; everyone in Hollywood knew that.

"With her," Todd went on, "she calls the shots, not the agent."

I could tell he was being defensive. Todd was not one of the biggest agents in town, and it might have even been the first time he had talked to Carolyn Barr. Very rarely did top casting people deal with small time agents.

"She saw you on a movie of the week," Todd explained. "And now you're under consideration for this new sit-com. Aren't you excited?"

"Of course, Bob," I said evenly. "Who wouldn't be? Which movie of the week was it?" I had done several, all one- and two-scene roles, but I was noticeable nevertheless, apparently.

"Honey," Todd's voice was rising, "how the hell do I know? I couldn't very well ask her that."

"Okay, okay," I smiled. "Tell me about the part. What kind of character is it?"

"What kind of character?" he repeated. "Listen, Claire, I have to hang up now; something important's just come up. Have Jim call me as soon as he gets in, okay?" He hung up before I could even answer.

"Whoopie!" I screamed, whirling around the room. I considered it a tremendous break. An interview with Carolyn Barr, and I was being considered for the second lead! I laughed, thinking of Robert Todd. He probably didn't even know what kind of part it was; he probably had been too afraid to ask Carolyn Barr any questions. Soon, I thought, I'll be with a better agent. I felt I was on an escalator that was moving slowly upward, toward the top. An escalator rather than a staircase, because it seemed that I didn't have to do very much but stand there in order to keep moving.

Jim came home and was just as excited as I was when he heard the news.

"What did I tell you, babe?" he said. "Now we're really moving."

He always thought in terms of we, but with me it was

always I. I didn't realize that until much later, of course.

My interview with Carolyn Barr was set up, and I took a full two-and-a-half hours to prepare myself. I made sure my makeup was flawless and not too heavy, and I wore a very classy green suit with an expensive white ruffled shirtwaist blouse under it. I had learned that when being interviewed by a woman it was better to play down my well-developed, sexy figure. What I hadn't yet learned was that Carolyn Barr was one of the most prominent lesbians in town.

When I walked into her office, big smile on my face, her eyes opened wide.

"Well," she said, "have a seat. Make yourself at home." She got up and walked over to a small bar at the side of her office. The bar was covered with some kind of hanging plant. "What are you drinking?"

"Oh, just some 7-Up, thank you Ms. Barr," I replied. It was only 9:30 in the morning.

"Sure," she said, and fixed herself a brandy over ice, the 8-ounce glass filled to the brim.

She handed me my 7-Up and sat down in her big swivel chair, leaning back and appraising me without speaking for several minutes. I tried not to become uncomfortable, but I did anyway and tried not to let it show.

"I've been seeing a lot of you lately," she said slowly, "and I'd like to see a lot more. On TV, I mean," she added.

I returned the smile. The woman was impeccably dressed, not at all masculine in her demeanor. It really never occurred to me that she was gay.

We talked for a while, just small talk, like where I grew up, when did I first decide to be an actress, and so on. Then she opened a drawer of her beautifully carved mahogany desk and pulled out some papers.

"No offense," she smiled, "but I would like you to read this scene with me. I've already seen your work, but I always get a lot out of hearing an actress read this scene."

"Of course," I agreed. "May I have a moment to look it over?"

"No," she said, "I prefer you to read it cold. You'll warm up to it as you go along." She smiled again.

Ice cold readings always scared me, but I agreed.

"Don't read it sitting down," she instructed. "Stand up."

I began to read. There were about 6 or 7 pages, and I didn't realize until I was halfway through the second page that it was a seduction scene between two women. I read the part of the passive, beautiful young girl, she the aggressive one.

"Don't be afraid," she read her lines in a husky voice, "I won't hurt you. I'm very gentle — very, very gentle."

As she got up and walked slowly around her desk toward me, I read ahead. To go through with this "scene," all I'd have to do would be to stand there and let her do whatever she wanted with my body. I had lines like, "Oh, that feels so good," and "Please, please don't stop."

I could have put down the script and left the office, but I was amused more than repelled. It was only a script, anyway, and I knew I was no lesbian. So what, I thought, let the old broad get her jollies. What's the harm, I figured. And last, but by far not least, I might get a damn good part out of it.

She opened my blouse and put her hand inside, caressing my breasts, moving her hand up and down my thighs under my skirt with the other. Finally she threw both scripts down on the floor and led me toward a sofa in a dimly lit corner of the room, where she made love to me with her hand and tongue until she had an orgasm. It didn't feel bad at all; not as good as making it with a guy, but not repulsive, like I would have thought.

She stood with her back to me, and I got dressed. Then

she turned and smiled, pouring herself more brandy and more 7-Up for me.

"Are you sure you don't want anything stronger?" she asked.

"No, thanks," I replied. "Seven-Up is fine."

"Now let's talk about your part in the new sit-com," she said, all-business, sitting down at her desk. "You play the pretty girl next door to a couple of newlyweds. The husband thinks you're a smash, but wouldn't dream of doing anything about it, yet the wife is jealous. Plenty of room for hilarious situations to develop."

"Yes," I smiled. Actually, I hated situation comedies; I thought they were the most ridiculous things I'd ever seen, and this sounded like no exception.

Carolyn Barr opened another drawer in her desk and took out a couple of 30-page scripts in binders.

"Here are the first two episodes. We start shooting in about five weeks. I'm co-producer on this one, by the way, and I think it'll really sell. And you'll be terrific," she added, looking into my eyes.

I hoped she wasn't getting turned on again, but if she was, I was prepared to accommodate her. I held in my trembling hand the first two scripts for the vehicle which would make me a star! What did I care whether I had sex with this dyke or not? It certainly was a low price to pay for fame and fortune.

CHAPTER 13

Taping started for my big show, and it was a wonderful experience, even though I didn't like the lead actor very much. He was very uptight and temperamental, and he had a terrible habit of trying to direct the other actors. But the director was very nice, and so was everyone else. Carolyn Barr would show up on the set every now and then, and she kept her eyes on me almost the whole time she was there. It didn't bother me a bit; in fact, it was kind of flattering. The other actress, the one who played the newlywed, was kind of envious of me, because after all, Carolyn Barr was a powerful person in the industry. A rumor started that Ms. Barr had the hots for me, and I denied it adamantly, even though it was obviously true.

When I told Jim about my one experience with Carolyn Barr, it seemed to excite him.

"Well, what do you expect, babe?" he said. "You could turn on a piece of stone, you sexy thing."

Now that I was co-star of a series, Jim hired a publicist, and my name began to appear in every column in Hollywood. We began to get offers from top agents, especially after Jim bought a full page ad in *Variety*, the Hollywood trade paper. It was a full-length photo of me, with congratulations from the network on their new star.

Jim paid off Robert Todd, after having a big argument with him about the amount.

"Thief, that's what he is!" Jim fumed. "What the hell does he expect? You've outgrown him. He can't do anything more for you, and he's made plenty of money off you this year."

It was true, but I could see the agent's point. As soon as a performer moved up, he or she dumped the agent that had first helped him get there and went on to an agency that could get him bigger and better parts and, of course, more money. It wasn't exactly fair, but that's the way it was done in Hollywood. There was no loyalty.

I signed with one of the top agents in town, and soon I started getting offers to do guest spots on talk shows. That I really liked, even more than acting. I didn't have to learn any lines. All I had to do was be myself, and I started getting fan mail. I answered each and every letter, sending along an autographed 8 x 10 glossy photo of myself, and I saved all the letters in a big box. All the reading I had done at the Hollywood Library in those first days in Hollywood was now paying off. I could converse on just about any subject, and people admired and respected me. Some actors and actresses who go on talk shows can only talk about one subject: acting. I had seen talk shows like that and I thought they got kind of boring. And I was always good at telling anecdotes; that went over in a big way when I did guest spots. I was having the time of my life!

Jim and I moved to a much more expensive apartment in Beverly Hills. He gave me the older Mercedes he had been driving and bought himself a new Lincoln Continental.

"Since I'm the star," I joked, "how come I don't get the new car?"

"Babe," he said patiently, "you can drive the Lincoln

whenever you want. But it's better for your image right now to drive the older Mercedes."

"Who says so?" I teased.

"Al, the publicity guy," he replied seriously. "And he's tops in the field, you know that. Next year when you're even bigger, we'll trade in the old Mercedes and get you a new one, or a Mazarati. 'Too-much-too-soon' is not a good image for a rising young star."

It made sense, but I found out later that other top publicists would have felt differently. Publicists see everything in terms of angles, and I guess it just depends on what angle they happen to view a given situation from. Apparently, there is no one right way of doing things. Of course, that seems to be true of life in general, doesn't it?

One day, after taping the seventh or eighth episode of "Next Door Bride" (that was the name of my sit-com, ridiculous, right?), I was walking toward the parking lot and noticed a black man standing off to one side, turned away from me so that I couldn't see his face. Somehow, he looked familiar anyway, and I slowed my step. As I walked by him, he turned away so that I still couldn't see his face. I kept going, figuring that I probably was mistaken, when suddenly I stopped, frozen in my tracks.

"Mary Clarissa," the deep, familiar voice called out. "May I still call you that?"

I turned to face William, standing there looking at me, but I couldn't read the expression on his face.

"William," I said, stepping forward. "What are you doing here?" I couldn't think of anything else to say.

He smiled slightly, but I could see hostility in it. "I work here, remember? In the mailroom. A guy's got to make a living, especially a struggling actor."

I just nodded, embarrassed.

"I'm not keeping you, am I?" he asked with a trace of sarcasm. "I mean, is your personal manager waiting for you? I wouldn't want to make you late."

I was getting very uncomfortable. "Yes," I lied, "and I've got to go now. But it was very nice seeing you again."

I turned and walked quickly to my car, started it up and drove out of the far end of the parking lot, so as not to have to drive past William.

For the next few days, I was disturbed. Jim noticed it.

"What's the matter, babe?" he asked. "Someone giving you a hard time on the set?"

"Sort of," I said. "Nothing important."

He grabbed me roughly. "Just tell me who it is," he snarled. "I'll have it taken care of."

This surprised me. I didn't know what he meant. "It's nothing," I replied. "Don't get so angry."

"I'm not joking, Claire. We're doing pretty good now, and I can afford a lot of things that I couldn't afford before. If anyone gives you a hard time, you just let me know."

"I don't like the way that sounds, Jimbo," I told him. I have always abhorred violence, and that sounded like what he meant.

"I'm not asking you, babe, I'm telling you!" He waved his finger in my face. "You just perform; let me take care of the rest."

It seemed the more successful I became, the more arrogant he got. He always had been a bully, but now he was becoming unbearable.

He swaggered out of the room, the big macho man, and I dismissed him and his antics from my mind. I had more important things to do than think about Jim, whom I had never really respected too much anyway. I had work to do, lines to learn for the next day's taping. Jim had helped me a lot, but not through talent, through his network of drug dealing. He had only one talent: he was great in bed. Not that I didn't appreciate his help or his lovemaking, for I did. But his love for me was the kind one reserves for possessions, not people. I suppose, though, that was about all he was capable of. Jim Robinson was not the kind of man I could ever love or feel very much for. But I didn't spend too much time thinking about it.

Soon the taping of all the episodes of "Bride Next Door" was completed, and I was in big demand as a guest on television talk shows, daytime ones, at least. The producers, especially Carolyn Barr, were really pushing it, because every time I guested on the talk shows, I of course plugged our show. They really thought our show was very good. I thought it was terrible. The jokes weren't a bit funny, and bordered on the insipid.

"So what?" Jim said to me. "Some of the most successful situation comedies are stupid. The viewers don't know the difference anyway. Put a laugh track on there and they'll laugh. The main thing is that they find one character on the show that they like, then pow! The show's a howling success."

He said it like it was his own idea, but I knew he had read it in TV Guide, because I had read the same article. All I hoped was that I would be the one the audiences loved.

We had taped all the episodes with a studio audience, and I must say I got a terrific reaction from them. I was experienced enough by now to be able to feel whether the audience was with me as I performed, and they were with me, at least most of them were, most of the time. I would get all kinds of fan letters backstage — propositions, even two proposals of marriage and one note from a pervert whom the studio guard promptly threw out of the studio. The guard walked me to my car after the taping that day, in case the creep was still lurking about.

At the beginning of the next season, they started airing "Bride Next Door." Jim and I sat together, drinking champagne, watching it on our new color console. It was the greatest feeling to see my name come on the screen in star billing, even though I was only third of the main three co-stars.

When I appeared on the screen, Jim seemed to be mesmerized. I was his product, his property, and he was so proud.

"Babe," he said, "you're terrific! Absolutely terrific!"

I did look good, and I got many more closeups than the other two co-stars, but I winced every time I heard the stupid, unfunny lines coming out of my mouth.

About an hour after the show was over, there was a knock at the door. It was a delivery boy with *two* dozen beautiful long-stemmed red roses. The card read simply: "To Claire, with much love, Carolyn."

The next day, she phoned at around 10 a.m.

"Claire, babe, you were fantastic, absolutely fantastic!" she gushed into the phone.

I wondered what she wanted; I knew she had seen screenings of all the episodes before they were aired.

"Thank you," I said, "and the flowers were beautiful."

"I'm glad you liked them," Carolyn said. "It's the least I could do for my new star. The show's a hit, you know. Another "All In The Family!"

"Wow," I said, "I sure hope you're right."

"Of course I'm right," she answered a bit harshly. "I've been getting phone calls all morning telling me how great it is. And a lot of praise for you, too, young lady."

Sure, I thought, all the ass-kissers in Hollywood wanted to get in good with Carolyn Barr. They'd tell her anything she wanted to hear. But comparing a piece of drivel like "Bride Next Door" to a fine show like "All In The Family" made me want to retch. But I had enough ego to assume that the people who told her I was good really meant it. Believe me, in Hollywood it really is easy to fall into the flattery trap.

I did get plenty of fan mail, though, sincere praise from viewers who really seemed to like me. Jim said that if it kept up, we could hire a secretary to answer it all.

"No way," I said adamantly. "I answer it all myself."

"Suit yourself," he shrugged. More money for him.

"I'd sooner have a secretary to answer the likes of Carolyn Barr and some of these other industry phones," I said hotly. "The fans are sincere. The big shots sure aren't."

This made him angry. "You just watch your mouth, little girl," he yelled. "Where the hell were all your fans before you met these so-called industry phonies? Tell me that! And, while we're on the subject, where were all your fans before you met these so-called industry phonies? Tell me that! And, while we're on the subject, where were all your adoring fans before you met me?"

He did have a point, but I didn't get a chance to answer.

"All you had then were two jerk-off fans," he raged on, "your old lady and that loser you were going to marry!"

I blew up. "Don't you ever, ever talk that way about them! My mother was a fine person, and as far as William, you wouldn't make a pimple on his ass!!"

What I said shocked me even more than it did him. I didn't know what made me say it; it had just popped out. I could see murderous rage in his eyes. I jumped up and before he could do anything about it, grabbed my purse which luckily was right by the door, and ran out of the house.

I jumped in the old Mercedes, found the keys quickly, started it up and screeched out of the driveway. I expected Jim to be following me any minute, so I drove fast.

Soon I found myself back in Hollywood, about 25 minutes drive from where we lived in Beverly Hills. I drove along Hollywood Boulevard. The traffic moved slowly, and I got a chance to reminisce a little. I passed a cheap little restaurant where William and I had sat for hours over hamburgers and weak coffee. I looked out the window and spotted Lerner's, where I used to buy most of my clothes, even my wedding dress. Those days seemed like a liftime ago. I turned left on Bronson and rode a block north to Franklin, then headed straight for the little French restaurant that served crepes, which my mother had liked so well.

I took a table in the rear, ordered some wine and a plate of strawberry crepes and just sat there, sipping the white wine and picking at the crepes for over an hour. I tried to understand why, when I had everything I'd said I wanted, I was so bitter and miserable. Remember, it's very difficult to see yourself as others see you, and I didn't really have any close friends to confide in.

I left the restaurant and drove slowly along Franklin. It was a clear night and I could see the eerie dome of the Griffith Park Observatory, high above the city in the Hollywood Hills.

I made another left onto the street that would take me up to the Observatory. I drove slowly along the sharply curved road to the Observatory. I parked the car and got out. It was 10 p.m. by now, and the Observatory was closed. There were some people; some were tourists, others lonely people like myself.

I stood at the edge of the cliff and looked down at the twinkling lights of the city. It felt good to be high above it all. Somehow being up there gave everything a different perspective. Then I looked up at the sky, with all the shiny stars, and realized that I wasn't so high up, after all. It was all relative.

Suddenly a voice, not two feet away from my face, said, "Ma'am?"

I almost jumped out of my skin. I hadn't heard anyone approaching. When I got over being startled, I looked around and saw a rather short man standing there. He didn't move, just stood there looking at me.

"Well, what is it?" I said with annoyance.

"Ma'am, aren't you Claire Stevens? I thought I recognized you, and I'm sorry I frightened you, but could I have your autograph?"

I relaxed and smiled. "Sure," I said kindly. I never could resist a fan.

The man broke into a big grin and pulled out a pen and paper, handing it to me.

"Anything in particular you'd like me to write?" I asked him.

"I don't know," he said shyly. "You can write, 'to John.' Then anything you like would be wonderful. And of course, your name."

I wrote the old standby, "To John, with best regards always, Claire Stevens." Then I handed it back to him.

He stood there studying the scrap of paper as though it were a thousand dollar bill as I walked toward my car.

On the way down the winding road, I noticed that a car was following me close behind. Soon the car's horn sounded. I stopped.

It was John, the fan. He walked over to my car and stooped down, his face at the level of my rolled down window.

"I saw you get in your car and drive off," he said, "and I decided to escort you down the hill. It's very unsafe for a woman to be out here alone this late at night . . ."

Sometehing about him was beginning to give me the willies.

". . . my wife was murdered you know . . ." his voice rose in pitch, ". . . raped and bludgeoned to death by a man whom the police never caught . . ."

That did it. I reached over quickly, threw the car into "drive" and stepped on the gas, leaving him behind in a cloud of dust. I tore around the curves much too fast, in a state of near panic. When I reached the bottom of the hill, I felt safer, surrounded by all the traffic. I saw a police car and almost flagged them down, thinking maybe I should report the man up there. But I stopped myself. What the hell could I tell them? He hadn't done anything, and I didn't even have his license number, nor a clear description of his car. I decided against telling the police about him and kept on driving. It was odd, I thought, when I was nearly raped in that little park years ago, I never even thought of calling the police. Now I had been considering reporting a man who had done nothing, just because he gave me the creeps.

A week later, though, I saw on the news that the police had discovered the dead body of a young black woman, not too far from the Observatory. A chill went up my spine. I went to the police station and gave them the information about "John," just in case he was the one who did it. They didn't get too excited about it, but showed me mug shots, none of which was "John." One of the cops got me a cup of coffee, and when no one was looking, asked me for my autograph. I thought it was strange the way people reacted to me, now that I was a well-known actress. But I loved all the attention, I'll tell you that!

After I decided against flagging down the police car, I drove around aimlessly for half an hour, trying to figure out where to go. I could have rented a motel room, but I didn't feel like being alone. I definitely couldn't go home, not until Jim cooled off. Somehow, I found my way to Stan and Mae's.

There was a light in the window, so I parked and knocked on their door. Stan opened the door and was obviously surprised and delighted to see me.

"Mary Clarissa!" he exclaimed. "Mae," he yelled back into the apartment. "Get some clothes on! Mary Clarissa's here!"

"I hope I'm not interrupting anything," I said slyly.

"No, no, no," he told me, "nothing important, that's

for sure!" He winked. "Well, don't just stand there, come on in!"

Mae came into the room, tying the belt on her bathrobe. "Mary Clarissa!" She threw her arms around me. "I'm so happy to see you!"

"To what do we owe the honor of this visit?" asked Stan, already getting drinks ready.

It was such a nice feeling. I had just dropped in out of nowhere, after 11 at night, and they were both delighted to see me.

"To tell you the truth, I had a fight with your friend Jim!" I said.

They both laughed.

"So if I could just borrow your sofa to sleep on tonight, I'll go home tomorrow, when he's cooled off," I explained.

"Well, you're more than welcome," Mae said. "I'll get you some fresh towels even!"

"Are you kidding?" Stan said. "I don't think we have any; Mae hasn't done the laundry in two weeks."

Mae made a face. "Oh, shut up, Stan."

"No kidding, Mary Clarissa, you can stay here as long as you like. Jimbo's a great guy, but I know he can get a little rough."

Mae and Stan exchanged a glance.

"I think we should tell her," Mae said, and Stan shrugged.

"Tell me what?!" I was alarmed. "What's going on?"

"He was already here looking for you," Mae said. "But I think you'll be safe enough. I don't think he'll be back."

"Naw," Stan agreed. "He thinks you're with your boyfriend."

"What boyfriend?!"

"You know," Stan said, "what's-his-face, that dude you were going to marry."

"William," I said softly.

"Yeah, William," Stan went on. "He assumed you were with William."

"He tried to find out where William lives; he wanted us to tell him," Mae said, "and he had that goon with him."

"What goon!?" I yelled.

"Tommy," she said, "or Tony, I don't remember. Must be seven foot tall. He does a lot of Jimbo's dirty work for him."

"It's Tommy," I moaned, "the gorilla. You didn't tell him where William lives?"

"How could we?" said Stan. "We don't even know."

"That's right," I said. "I don't even know where he lives anymore. Oh God, what have I gotten myself into?"

"You're a star now, Mary Clarissa, or should we call you Claire?" Stan's eyes glowed with admiration and a trace of envy. "What else matters?"

"Oh, for heaven's sake, Stan!" I snapped. "There are other things that count, too. I'm still a person, believe it or not!"

Stan didn't bat an eye. He had been trying for so many years to make it as a musician, to make in Show Biz. He couldn't imagine anything else mattering if someone was a star.

I stayed awake most of the night, trying to figure out what my next move would be. In the morning, I called Jim.

"Oh, baby," he said, "where the hell are you? I've been worried sick!"

"I'm fine," I said. "I needed time alone, to think. I stayed in a motel."

"What motel? Where? Stay right where you are, I'll come get you."

"No," I said, "I'll be home soon."

"Why don't you want me to come?" he yelled. He probably thought I was with William.

"Because I have my own car, remember? I'll be home soon."

"Oh, that's right," he said almost apologetically. "I guess I'm just not thinking."

No kidding, I thought. "Well, I'll be home soon, hon," I said softly, feeling more like spitting in his face.

I said goodbye to Mae and Stan and thanked them again.

"I hope we see you again in the near future," Mae said, kissing me on the cheek.

"I'll come by, I promise," I told her.

"Well, see you on the silver screen, anyway!" Stan grinned.

When I got home, Jim was waiting for me, all hugs and kisses. He took me right to bed, and I closed my eyes, imagining he was someone else. No one in particular, just anyone but Jim. When it was over, he fell asleep, and I got up and took a shower. I just couldn't stand him anymore.

In a couple of hours, he got up and went out.

"I'll be back in a few hours," he told me, kissing me goodbye. "I've got some business to take care of."

"Right," I agreed sweetly.

The moment he was gone I went into the bedroom and packed my things. Then I drove to the bank and took out $5,000 in cash. From there I went to the Valley and drove around, looking for signs saying "Apartment for Rent." I finally found what I was looking for on a small street in North Hollywood.

The manager, a little old woman, wrote out a receipt for first and last month's rent plus cleaning fee. The whole amount came to less than $500; rents were still cheap in L.A. at the time (and it wasn't so long ago, either).

As she handed me the receipt, she pushed her glasses down on her nose and stared. "Don't I know you from somewhere?" she asked.

I shrugged. "I doubt it, Mrs. Melendez," I said. "Must

be someone who looks like me." I had used the name Mary Claire, so at least she wouldn't see my name listed in TV Guide.

I went into my new apartment and unpacked, then went to a pay phone and called my answering service.

"There's a message from a Carolyn Barr," the operator told me.

I returned Carolyn's call immediately.

"Hi, Claire!" she said briskly. "I have good news and bad. Which do you want first?"

"Take your pick," I mumbled.

"Okay, let's get the bad news out of the way. The show's been cancelled.

"What?!" I exclaimed.

"Yeah, I know, it's terrible. The lead actor was in an auto accident last night; you'll see it in today's papers. He was messed up pretty badly, won't be able to work for at least a year. The network execs are afraid to replace him; they'd rather cancel, even though we've been doing pretty good in the ratings. They're such a bunch of cowards," she said with contempt. "You're the real star of the show, anyway."

I knew that was true; the actor had always been jealous of me. Now that he was hurt, I felt bad for him. "Well, it would be hard to have another actor take over his character. The public might not accept it."

"Right, right, right," Carolyn said. She always took things in stride, knowing what could be changed and what couldn't. "But now on to bigger and better things. The good news is that an associate of mine, a producer, is very interested in you. You see, we're going to do a daytime talk show, and we both agree that you'd be perfect as host. How does that sound?"

"My own show?" I said dumbly. "Well, Carolyn . . ." I was speechless.

"Tut, tut, my dear," she went on, "you have all day to

think it over. You're to be at my home tonight for dinner, my associate will be there. Now take down the address."

I rummaged through my purse for pen and paper as she rattled off the Bel Air address.

"And feel free to bring your, uh, husband," she went on coyly.

I decided to take a chance and trust her. "Carolyn, Jim is not my husband; you know that. Besides, I've left him. Of course, you won't say anything to anybody . . ."

There was a pause. "Of course not, Claire. You know me better than that!" She sounded delighted. "Now I need to know where you're staying, of course."

"We'll talk about it tonight," I told her, and hung up.

I had been in Hollywood too long to get overly excited over an offer until the contract was signed, sealed and delivered. But I couldn't help but feel thrilled as I pictured myself hosting my own show.

I went back to my new apartment and arranged the living room as though it were the set of a talk show. I pretended there was this guest and that, and interviewed them all. It might sound crazy, but actors do this all the time, and it helps when you get out there in front of the camera, sort of like a private rehearsal.

Then I decided to take a nap, since I had hardly slept at Stan and Mae's. I was beginning to feel exhausted, and I wanted to look terrific at dinner tonight. I wondered whether Carolyn's "associate" was male or female.

I hope it's another dyke, I thought, and one whom she's interested in. That way, she would be more likely to leave me alone. I had enough complications in my life right now without Carolyn Barr. But the way my luck had been going, it would probably be some old guy with hot pants, and then I'd have both of them to contend with. My professional life was in great shape, but my personal life was becoming a shambles.

CHAPTER 14

The dinner at Carolyn Barr's went much better than I could have hoped. Carolyn had a companion there, a lovely redheaded girl who was about seventeen and looked thirteen. The producer, a prominent man in the industry, came with his middle-aged wife, and everyone treated me very well. After a while it became clear to me that both Carolyn and the producer had their minds set on me as the hostess for the daytime talk show they were planning to produce.

When it was time to leave, the producer said to me, "It was such a pleasure meeting you, Claire. Carolyn will get in touch with your agent within the next few days, and I'm sure a deal can be worked out. We plan to get this thing off the ground in about eight or ten weeks."

No mention was made during the evening of my "personal manager," and I was grateful for that.

When I was getting ready to go home, Carolyn put her arm around the young redhead and said, "Claire, the night is still young. Why don't you stay and have a little nightcap with us?" It was not a request. She was pretty much telling me to stay.

"Well, just a quick one," I replied.

Into three ornate glasses she poured some sweet,

expensive, awful-tasting liqueur and we sat there sipping it, making small talk.

After a while, Carolyn went over to the girl, a shy, passive type, and began to make love to her, all the while looking at me. Instinctively, I got up to leave, but Carolyn said, "No, babe. Please stay where you are." Apparently she wanted me as an audience. I couldn't see what harm there could be, so I sat back down and watched them making it, first on the couch, then on the thick red carpet. When everything was over and they both lay on the floor exhausted, I saw an opportunity to make my exit.

"See you later," I said from the door. Then I was outside before Carolyn could answer.

The next morning, I put on some very plain clothes, wrapped a paisley scarf around my head and went out to a pay phone to check my service. There were four messages from Jim, "Urgent," they said, and one from my agent.

I disregarded Jim's messages — I wasn't ready to deal with him yet — and called my agent.

"Claire," he said, "where can I reach you if I have to? Something big is about to break for you, probably within the next week or so."

I was surprised. He apparently already knew that Jim and I had broken up. There was no contract between Jim and myself, so legally I was free of him as personal manager.

"I'll call you every day," I said, avoiding the issue of where I was staying, "twice a day if you like."

"Good enough," he said, and hung up.

I went to a small TV store on Ventura Boulevard and purchased a little portable black and white television set. If I was going to be a talk show hostess, I was going to watch every talk show I could, every day. Of course I loved being a star, but I also wanted to do my very best work.

The next day, I finally got up enough nerve to call Jim. I really was afraid of him by now.

"Oh, babe!" he said into the phone. "I miss you so much. These last few days have been absolute hell on earth for me. Are you ready to come back?"

That was strange, I thought. He was talking as though I had something to say in the running of my life.

"No," I told him quietly. "I need some time by myself. I've been under a lot of pressure lately, and I've got to get my head together. You'll see, it's for the best."

"I understand," he replied. "But just as soon as you're ready, let me know." There was a click on the other end, and he was gone.

I was very confused. That definitely was not the way anyone who knew Jim would expect him to react. What the hell could he be up to, I wondered suspiciously. Well, there wasn't too much I could do about it, so I put Jim and my problems with him out of my mind, and began to concentrate all my energies on preparing to be a talk show hostess.

Within a couple of weeks, the talk show deal was set.

"We had expected it to go through a lot sooner," Carolyn told me over lunch at a swank Beverly Hills restaurant, "but the network guys, quite frankly, were scared of having a black hostess." She shook her head from side to side contemptuously. "Cowards," she said with disgust, "that's all they are, a bunch of gutless wonders. Why, if I had had as little nerve as any of them, I'd still be in the typing pool at Columbia Pictures."

That was where she'd started in this town, I had heard, and she had manipulated her way to the top of the heap ruthlessly, playing on every angle, every weakness she detected in those who could help her. One time, gossip had it, one of the studio heads had the hots for her, not in spite of her being a lesbian, but because of it. She calculatedly put him off at first, then gradually acted like she was warming up to him, and finally had a full blown affair with him which made the gossip columns. He was delighted, thinking he had "converted" her, and rewarded her with plenty of power. That was the type of thing she did and did well. I have to admit that I did admire her, in a way, ruthless though she was. She had a lot more nerve than I did, although I was doing pretty well myself for an uneducated black girl from the slums of Saginaw, Michigan.

"So," Carolyn was saying, nibbling at her avocado and shrimp salad, "the best we could do was to get it on locally to start. When you start to click with the public, the sponsors will be beating a path to the network's door, and we're sure to go national."

"But what if I don't click?" I asked realistically.

"Don't worry, you will. You'll automatically have the black audience; even if you weren't any good, you'd have them. But you are good, and you'll have a lot of us whites as well, especially the men," she added, unable to stop herself from staring at my well-formed breasts. If you wanted to kow what men would go for, she was a good one to ask!

I smiled demurely, but couldn't resist leaning forward slightly, giving her an eyeful — I was wearing a V-neck blouse. Personally, I thought the whole business of women making it with women was second rate. Give me a man anytime, I thought.

Once the contracts for the show were signed, I totally immersed myself in preparation, watching every daytime and nighttime talk show on television, and reading up on every imaginable topic, everything from physics to gourmet cooking. I felt I needed to know a little about a lot of subjects; you never could tell whom they would line up for a guest appearance on my show. I suppose I was overdoing it, but I enjoyed it. I suppose it took my mind off my mixed-up personal life, and my worries about Jim.

He had made no attempt to get in touch with me or see me, other than an occasional message on my answering service, which I would sometimes return, sometimes not. It was out of character for him and it scared me.

Another thing that scared me was that I sometimes found myself thinking about William, and began to have dreams about him quite frequently. Try as I might, I couldn't shut him out of my mind. And the last thing I wanted to do was face the possibility that I was still in love with him, after all this time. It could never work out, I told myself, not now. I was a star, and rapidly rising, and I didn't think he would ever be able to tolerate that. He was, after all, a gifted actor, but unsuccessful. How could he help but resent me? Why it never occurred to me that I might be in a position to help his career, I don't know. It was probably selfishness on my part. I tended to think in terms not of helping others, but of having them help me. I suppose I had strong dependency needs, common with women in our culture, Women's Lib notwithstanding.

Another factor was the danger William would probably be in if I took up with him again. Jim was an insecure, jealous man, and I shuddered to think of the violence and destruction he was capable of, if provoked. To him, people were objects to be used, enjoyed, tossed away if no longer useful, and destroyed if they got in his way. If made aware of this, I was sure he would have all kinds of justification for his behavior, but I doubted if he thought about it at all, anyway. He was not the introspective type.

The schedule for the taping of my show was sent to me by messenger, and soon the first day of work arrived. I must say, I was a nervous wreck. I got to the studio nearly two hours before before I was supposed to be there, and this made quite an impression on everybody involved. When a bit player arrives much too early, anyone who happens to notice thinks she's simply "insecure." I had had that experience. But when the star arrives hours early, she's admired as a "real person."

Carolyn was on the set, full of well wishes for me, and the morning taping went smoothly. I had lunch with her in the commissary.

"Claire, you're doing a terrific job, just as I knew you would," she said delightedly. Then she gave me pointers on what I was doing that she liked, and what she thought could be improved. "Of course, those are only suggestions," she said tactfully. "You're doing great, really."

I knew that when Carolyn made a "suggestion," the "suggestee" had better follow through. I fully intended to do so. Actually, her advice was quite good. She certainly knew her business, and I gave her credit for that. There were powerful people in Hollywood who just liked to throw their weight around, most of the time not knowing the first thing about what they were talking about. They surrounded themselves with yes-men and nobody dared disagree with them for fear of being ruined in the industry. Carolyn was not that type of person. Her power was backed up by talent and intelligence.

Strange, I thought, sitting there listening to her talk about the show, she was one of the few people in Hollywood I could admire, and she had to be a full-blown dyke. Of course, I realize that sexual perference has nothing to do with it, but I suppose at the time I was prejudiced. Where I came from in Michigan, if someone was gay, he or she would make sure to keep it a deep, dark secret, hoping against hope the word wouldn't get out. It was more socially acceptable to do violence than to go to bed with someone of your own sex. It was better to be a criminal than to be gay. I guess I was still rooted in my early training, more so than I realized.

Carolyn and I walked back to the set together, and when I walked through the heavy iron door, I stopped cold. A few feet away, standing there grinning, was Jim Robinson.

Carolyn smiled at him, whispering to me between clenched teeth, "Take it easy, hon, there's not going to be any trouble. Everything's taken care of. Trust me."

I began to feel faint as he approached us, striding over nonchalantly, still smiling. How the hell had she taken care of anything, I thought angrily. She should have had him barred from the set!

"Ladies, ladies," Jim was saying pleasantly. He kissed us on the cheek, first me, then Carolyn. "I'm sorry I couldn't make it here this morning, some important business came up. But I'm here now, and I can't wait to see the rest."

I noticed he was wearing a very expensive suit, one I had never seen before. His hair was styled impeccably, as though he had gone to the most exclusive hair stylist in Beverly Hills. He really looked good, and he didn't seem the least bit angry or jealous, although he kept his eyes on me at all times. I couldn't imagine what was going on. Had he found someone else to possess? Was I finally free of him? I certainly hoped so.

The afternoon taping went well, after I got over my self-consciousness about Jim's presence on the set. At any minute, I expected him to pull something. He was so hard and mean. But nothing of any consequence happened, and so I drove home at the end of the day, exhausted, making sure I wasn't being followed.

We taped all that week, enough for the following week's air time. There was plenty of publicity, even a full-length feature on me with plenty of photos in the Sunday entertainment section of a major L.A. paper. The article told of my humble beginnings in Saginaw, Michigan, the fact that I came from a broken home, and went on in glowing terms about my mother and her tragic death. Most of it was true, but very, very cleaned up. In the article I always came out on top of things. I wished it were true in real life; even though I was not a star, I never had the feeling I was on top of anything. I was still plagued by the same insecurities and fears I had always had, though I was happy about my success.

They quoted me as saying, "After my mother died, I knew I had to concentrate all my efforts on succeeding as a performer. I'm still young, and there's plenty of time for love, marriage and children."

I had never even given them an interview. In fact, the first I heard about it was when Carolyn told me to buy the paper on Sunday.

"I think you'll like what you see," she said with a big smile.

She was right; I did. I liked the way they presented my life; it sounded much better than the real thing.

"The scaredy-cats at the network will be deluged with plaudits for you," Carolyn informed me. "We'll see to that, of course."

I was a bit crestfallen. I had hoped people would write in of their own accord; I hadn't been aware that the fan mail would have to be beefed up.

Carolyn laughed heartily, intuiting my thoughts. "Of course, there will be plenty of real fan mail," she explained, "and some complaints, too. There always are complainers. But the more fan mail the network guys see, the stronger the position we'll be in. That's why we do it this way. Also, once the show is on the air, we have enough columnists in our corner who will keep informing the public how terrific it is. You know how so many viewers are, unable to decide what they like until some expert tells them what's good and what's not."

"I understand," I said in agreement.

"Well, don't look so down-in-the-mouth," Carolyn said, touching my hand. "That's the way it is in the real world, and it's not a personal offense against you. You have to accept reality, whether you like it or not."

"I've always been a realist," I said a bit defensively.

"Have you?" she replied. "That's good."

The doubt in the voice of this woman whom I so respected planted a seed of doubt in my own mind. Could it be I wasn't as in touch with what was going on as I thought I was? Soon, several factors in my life would converge, and I would realize just how little I knew myself and those around me.

CHAPTER 15

My local daytime talk show was soon a big success, high in the ratings, and after a couple of months we were offered an afternoon time slot on the network. The show would now be seen all over the country. My salary more than tripled, and some of the biggest celebrities badgered their agents to get them on as guests on my show. I wasn't prime time, like Johnny Carson, but I was pretty damn popular, although a few of the more cowardly network executives cringed when certain affiliate stations in the South refused to air my show. There wasn't enough of them to kill the deal, though, and soon I was busily preparing for my network show.

"What is there to prepare?" Carolyn said impatiently. "You just do exactly as you have been. The show will be the same; you'll simply have a larger audience."

"I don't agree," I told her. "With a national audience, I can't be as casual as I have been with a small local audience. And my guests will be more prominent. I have to handle them differently."

She got angry. "Now you listen to me," she said. "You don't handle them any differently. You don't change your personality one iota, do you understand? It's the secret of your success — your naturalness, your spontaneity, even if it has been rehearsed in your mind. Don't you dare mess us up by taking off on your own! You're just a performer, and I want you to do what you do best. Leave the decision-making to people who know what they're doing. In that area, you certainly don't!"

I was stunned and hurt. She had never talked to me that way before. No producer or director had.

"Is that so?" I asked angrily. "So I'm just a performer, a yo-yo, a trained seal? Is that what you think? Well, let me tell you something, lady! Without a performer you 'decision-maker' smartasses don't have a show!"

We were in an exclusive restaurant in Malibu, and I started to get up to leave. Heads began to turn in our direction.

"You keep your voice down, young lady," Carolyn hissed. "Don't you dare make a scene! Sit back down again slowly, and laugh quietly, as though you had been kidding."

I glanced quickly around, avoiding the eyes that were on me, then did as she said. "Why is it all right if you raise your voice?" I asked resentfully, but smiling.

"Because," she answered, also smiling, "I did not raise my voice. I know how to control my voice, and I'm not even an actress. You associate anger with shouting, so that was the impression you got. My voice was low and intense, and you were the only one who heard what I said."

I thought back a few minutes, and realized she was right. She had seemed furious, but no one knew it but me. Again, I had to give her credit. She was right, as usual.

Of course, I took Carolyn's advice and didn't change my style on the show when we switched to network television. But I continued to do my research on each guest and his or her topic, so that I could interview intelligently. If an author came on plugging a new book, I made sure to read the book. I went over their bio's with a fine tooth comb so I could gleen information on what kind of person I was dealing with. I would go over any information I received on what the guest wanted to talk about and familiarize myself with the particular topic. It took, in my opinion, more than beauty and sex to be, and more importantly, to remain, a star.

I loved being a TV talk show hostess. It was so much more rewarding and satisfying than being an actress. The viewers, I felt, got to know *me* personally, not some imaginary character a writer had concocted. It seemed like a much more honest aspect of performing. Remember, I didn't have very many close friends, if any. The viewers became my friends, especially the ones who wrote fan letters. I had many fans who wrote to me regularly, and I always answered the correspondence personally. To me, they were pen-pals.

A black teenage girl in Philadelphia wrote: "Dear Claire, I am so glad your show is on television. I admire you so much. Life here in our neighborhood is dreary and ugly, and you give me hope that someday I can raise myself out of here and be somebody important, like you. Some of my girl friends and I would like to start a fan club for you. Could you please let us know how we would go about doing something like that? Also, someday I hope to meet you in person. My mother knows I am writing you this letter and she says she is proud of me, that it's better to admire someone like you than to fawn over all those rock stars who take drugs and spend all their money foolishly. I hope to hear from you soon."

I was really moved by that letter, and I wrote back that I was delighted at her and her friends wanting to start a fan club for me. "It is really an honor," I told her in the letter. "I will forward your letter to my publicity people, because I don't know how to go about starting a fan club, either! I'm sure they will supply you and your friends with the necessary material. If you are ever in Los Angeles, perhaps a meeting can be arranged."

Then there were the nasty letters. One man wrote: "How does a black bitch like you get so all-fired high and mighty? How many men did you have to screw to get to where you are? Every time I see you interviewing some important person, asking them questions that are none of your black business, I want to puke. By the way, when are you going to have Governor George Wallace on your stupid show? Or don't you have the balls?"

I couldn't help but wonder why, if my show was so distasteful to him, did he watch it? I remembered back in the sixties, when Carol Doda introduced the first popular topless act, people used to climb high walls to peek in and see what she was doing, then they would promptly call the police and complain with moral outrage. I guess it was the same principal involved. Some people only feel alive when they've got something to complain about.

Then there were complaints that had nothing to do with my being black.

One woman in the Mid West wrote: "To Claire Stevens: It's women like you that make it hard for the rest of us normal women, who want nothing more than to stay home and take care of the house and be a good wife and mother. My husband insists on watching your boring show since he is home in the afternoon now that he is unable to work and is on disability. He constantly points you out to me as an example of what women can do if we want to. Well, I don't want to!" I guess she expected me to quit my career so that she could stay at home!

There was some vicious hate mail, too, luckily not too much, which I promptly turned over to my agent. He gave things like that to the police to keep on file in case anything ever came of it. Things like that scared me, but I put it in back of my mind. It was part of the game of being a star, I figured.

By and large, though, the mail I received was quite complimentary, to the point of being flattering. When the

Nielsen ratings came out, my show was Number One in its afternoon time slot. I thought about my mother often, and how happy she would have been to see her ambitions for me being fulfilled.

Still my personal life was boring and unhappy, and my sex life was nil. I had moved to a private house in Laurel Canyon, where a lot of celebrities lived, but I had no real friends to invite over to share it with me, and I was never one to get involved with hangers-on, those loveless souls who prey on the rich and famous, pretending to be their friends until they can find someone bigger to fawn on.

One evening, on impulse, I got dressed up, got into my new white Mazaratti and drove down the hill. At Sunset Boulevard, I turned right, driving farther out on the Strip. The traffic was moving slowly, so I had a chance to survey the night clubs, porno places and various watering holes that were populated by the flashy folks who lived life in the fast lane. Soon I came to a rather popular singles bar. With determination, I turned into the driveway and stepped out of my car as a valet stepped up and held the door open for me.

It was crowded and smoky in the bar as I made my way through the mass of lonely humanity and headed for the bar. I ordered a drink, having to shout to be heard above the noise and loud rock music in the large room. The bartender recognized me, but made no mention of it. By now, I could tell when someone recognized me from my show.

Soon, a good-looking young white guy came over.

"You're Claire Stevens, aren't you?" he said without fawning. "I recognized you the minute you walked in. Can I buy you a drink?"

"No, thanks," I replied. Tonight I didn't want to be recognized as a star, just a woman. "I'm waiting for someone."

"Oh, excuse me," he said politely, and vanished into the crowd.

I stayed at the bar for almost two hours. Every guy who came over knew who I was, and that wasn't what I wanted. I got up to leave, a little depressed.

Just then, a muscular, dark-complected black man walked up to me. "Leaving so soon?" he said. "I just got here. You're a nice-looking chick." He signalled the bartender. "What are you drinking?" he asked.

"Uh, screwdriver," I answered, "with lots of ice, tall glass." Maybe it was worth staying a little while longer.

He ordered our drinks.

"What's your name?" he asked. "I'm Chuck."

"Mary Clarissa," I told him.

"Do you come here often?"

"No," I said. "This is my first time."

"Yeah, mine too," he said facetiously. Apparently people who frequented singles bars weren't too proud of it.

"No, really," I said. "I'm a shy, lonely girl."

"You're a very beautiful girl, Mary Clarissa. But I suppose you already know that."

"Sure," I told him. "But it sounds better coming from you." He certainly was sexy, and I was getting very turned on.

"Drink up," he said. "We can go someplace more quiet, where we can relax."

We walked outside into the cool night air. "My, it's good to breathe again," I said, filling my lungs. "That place has more smoke than a fire."

"Right," he agreed, surveying my figure with pleasure. "It sure is."

The valet brought his car out, and just as I was getting in, I realized that I had left my silk change purse on the bar.

"I'll be right back," I said, and went back into the club.

It took a couple of seconds for my eyes to adjust to the dark from the bright lights of Sunset Strip; then I couldn't believe what I saw. I was standing maybe three feet away from Tommy, the gorilla. I rushed back out, jumped into Chuck's car.

"Let's get out of here, quick!" I told him without explanation.

He stepped on the gas and off we went.

"Where to?" he asked calmly.

"I don't know yet," I said, very agitated. "Listen, don't get alarmed, but I think we may be followed."

"We're not being followed," he replied. "I've been watching."

"You have?" I asked, surprised.

"Of course. Do you think I'm stupid?" He laughed. "You rush out of the bar and tell me to take off in a hurry, I'm going to make sure we're not being followed. I'm a lover, not a fighter, although I'm pretty good at both."

What could I say?

"Open the glove compartment," he told me.

I did. There sat a small gun. I was beginning to get nervous.

He noticed from the corner of his eye, and laughed again. "I work as a bodyguard," he said. "In my business, you have to protect yourself." He reached in his pocket and took out some I.D. that had his picture on it, saying he was a licensed private detective. "I moonlight," he explained.

I began to relax. "Well," I said, "I feel well protected."

"You still haven't told me where we're going," he commented casually.

I made a quick decision. "I live up in Laurel Canyon," I told him. "Let's go over there."

"Nice place you got here," he said when we walked in the door.

"Thanks," I replied. "Want a drink?"

"Sure," he said.

I fixed us both drinks and sat down next to him on the

sofa. He didn't waste any time getting right down to business.

He was a forceful, dynamic lover, and in his strong arms I reached the heights of ecstasy. We stayed in bed, or rather, on my plush velvet sofa, until three in the morning, making love over and over until I was so exhausted and sore that I could barely move.

Then he got up, got dressed and fixed himself a drink at my bar.

"Get dressed," he said, "I want to talk to you."

I did.

"Now," he said, "what kind of trouble are you in?"

"Never mind," I told him. "It's nothing, really. I don't want to talk about it."

"I know who you are," he interrupted. "I know you're Claire Stevens."

I was honestly surprised.

"I sat there and watched you turn down guy after guy, and realized that you didn't want to be recognized. So I acted accordingly."

"I see," I said slowly.

"I always wanted to screw a star," he said with a smile. "Especially a beautiful black one."

I stood up. "Get out," I told him.

"Oh, sit down, Claire. Can't you take a little joke? Now tell me what kind of trouble you're in."

I sat down and sipped at the drink I had left sitting there hours ago. It was flat, but I was thirsty and I didn't feel like getting up and fixing another.

"All right," I said, "I'll tell you all about it. But you've got to promise to keep it quiet." I realized I was taking a huge risk confiding in him, but I really felt like talking, unburdening myself. I told him everything, and it took nearly half an hour.

Chuck sat and listened patiently. When I was done

with my story, he said, "I'm prepared to offer you my services."

I couldn't resist smiling. "So besides being a bodyguard and detective, you're also a male hooker?"

"Hey, you do have a sense of humor," he laughed. "Actually, I meant my services as a bodyguard."

"I'll consider it," I said. "How much do you charge?"

"Five hundred a week, full time," he told me. "And I do accept bonuses every once in a while." He indicated the sofa with his eyes.

"How generous of you," I said dryly. I thought about it. What did I have to lose? He would be good protection in case Jim Robinson began acting up, five hundred dollars a week was nothing to me now, and the son-of-a-gun was one hell of a good lay.

"Okay," I said, "you got it. Do I have to sign a contract?"

"No," he replied. "Let's shake on it."

"Okay," I said, holding out my hand.

He reached out and took my hand, shook it, then with one quick motion pulled me against his strong body, holding me firmly there. He caressed my face, then ran his big hand down my neck and across my breasts. Then he kissed me hard, and as tired as I was, I was ready to make love again.

"That's the way I firm up deals with beautiful young women," he said. "By the way, I'm not a jealous man like your Jim Robinson. I hope you're the same way."

"I am," I told him. "There's no room in my life for jealousy."

"Good," he said. "Now, where can I stay? Have you got servant quarters?" he laughed.

It was a big house, and I set up a room for him in what I was using as a den, in the front part of the house.

"When do you want to start officially?" I asked.

"How about right now?" he said, removing the items from his trousers pocket, including a small gun, which he placed on a table.

Ignoring my presence, he got undressed, walked over and turned off the light, lay down on the couch and fell asleep. I left the room, closing the door behind me.

What had I gotten myself into now, I wondered.

CHAPTER 16

The next day at the studio, Carolyn approached me. There was fire in her eyes.

"I want to talk to you," she said, "in private."

They weren't ready for me yet, so we went out for a walk.

"What the hell were you doing at that singles place last night? Have you flipped your cork?" she said angrily.

"Oh, come off it, Carolyn," I answered impatiently. "I have a right to a little fun, you know."

"Damn it, Claire," she went on. "Don't you realize that the only reason Jim isn't bothering you is that he thinks you're having the affair of the century with me?"

My blank look was answer enough.

"Boy, you are naive," she said under her breath.

"I just assumed that you were paying him off," I replied coolly. "I understand he's been living it up lately."

"Are you kidding?" she sneered. "Pay my good money to a turkey like that? Only if I have to will I shell out of my own pocket. What I did was supply him with higher paying clients for his little business, lots of them. But even that wouldn't have prevented his jealous rages. You should know that better than me," she added.

As usual, she was right.

I decided to break the news. "In the singles bar," I told

her, "I ran into one of Jim's goons. Tommy, the gorilla."

"That's too bad," she said, not as upset as I thought she'd be.

"But I have a bodyguard now," I told her, waiting for the explosion, "a full-time, live-in bodyguard." I told her his name.

"Good," she said, "that might help."

I was amazed; this was not the reaction I expected.

"Now let's talk about something very important," Carolyn was saying, "to your career and mine. Jonathan Brown is in town and he wants to meet you."

Again, my blank expression betrayed my ignorance.

"Good God," she exclaimed, "don't you now anything?! Jonathan Brown is . . ."

"Good God, yourself!" I interrupted. I was getting sick and tired of her talking down to me. "I know plenty of things. I'm not stupid, and you know it, Ms. Big Shot Carolyn Barr, Small-Town-Girl-Makes-Good-In-The-Big-City!"

"All right, all right, Claire!" She held her hand up to silence the barrage. "I was just surprised that you don't know that Jonathan Brown is one of the biggies at the network in New York, and he's dying to meet you. I've arranged a date for tomorrow night."

"At your place?" I asked offhandedly.

"No," she said, "at his hotel room. He's staying at the Beverly Hills Hotel."

"What's that supposed to mean?" I said hotly. "I'm not some kind of high class call girl, Carolyn!"

"Now look," she said intensely. "If you're nice to him and he likes you the way I think he will, we might be able to get the show moved up to prime time. Do you know what that will mean to your career? He's already half in love with you and he hasn't even met you yet. He's really a biggie, Claire. He can make you a black female Johnny Carson!"

Suddenly my mind flashed back to the first night I met William, that little coffee shop we went to after acting class. I could hear him saying how he thought I would be great as a talk show hostess, and I told him how the networks were hardly looking for a black female ... Oh, how I wished I could turn the calendar back, back to the days when I was in love and happy, and William was my whole life. Tears began to well up in my eyes.

"Claire!" Carolyn brought me sharply back to the present. "Aren't you paying attention to what I'm saying? This is very important!"

"I know, I know," I replied. "You want me to go to bed with this big shot network dude from New York. Is he married?" I asked dejectedly.

She sighed. "Yes."

"Then forget it," I snapped.

"Oh, listen to Miss Self Righteous Morality," she snapped back. "Now just hear me out. His wife is in a sanitarium on Long Island. He certainly can't divorce her; she's dying of some long-term illness or other. But what do you expect him to do, become a monk?"

"I don't expect him to do anything, Carolyn," I replied. "But neither do I expect myself to become his playmate while his wife is dying."

Suddenly she turned cold. She looked at me with an expression I had never seen before, as though she were coming to the end of her rope.

"Do whatever you think is best, Claire," she said quietly, then turned and walked away from me.

I had a sinking feeling. I knew that in show business, you either went up or you went down; you couldn't pass up opportunities with impunity. And Carolyn was right. No one was indispensable. If I lost my footing there were plenty of beautiful young starlets, white and black, who were all too eager to step into my place.

I thought about it all through the day's taping. Maybe

it wasn't so terrible to sleep with this big shot network guy. If his wife was dying, she was dying, it was no one's fault. And it wouldn't be the same thing as having an affair with a married man and wrecking his home, the way my parents' marriage was wrecked.

During one of the breaks in the afternoon, I walked up to Carolyn.

"What time am I supposed to be at the Beverly Hills Hotel?" I asked.

She smiled. "Smart girl," she said, and I turned away. "Oh, come on, babe, chin up. He's not that terrible. He's expecting you at seven."

I drove there, with Chuck following in his car.

"Wait in the bar or something," I instructed him. "I'll be down in a couple of hours at the most."

On the way up in the elevator, I found myself thinking of William, wishing it were him I was meeting instead. Every time I was unhappy with something in my life, I would find myself thinking of him, and the happy, carefree, loving times we had known together.

I knocked at the door and Mr. Big Shot opened it. When he saw me, he stepped back a few paces, a look of awe on his face. Him, with all his money and power, in awe of me!

"Come in, Miss Stevens," he said. Clearly he was infatuated with me.

He was bland and unattractive, and even worse in bed. I pretended to enjoy myself. When I do things, I do them all the way, not half-assed.

Afterward, he talked to me about going on prime time.

"It would be great," he said enthusiastically. "You are the most beautiful, talented woman I have ever seen or known, and I've seen and known plenty of them."

I'll bet he has, I thought.

"Are you going to be on the West Coast long?" I asked, hoping he wasn't.

"Yes," he said happily. "At least three months, on business. And I hope to be seeing a lot of you, Miss Stevens."

Miss Stevens, he called me, after we had just spent over half an hour in bed! Ugh!

"Of course," I answered sweetly. William, I thought, William, come back to me. Take me away from all this.

I left Mr. Big Shot's suite and found Chuck waiting in the hallway.

"Come on, bodyguard," I said, "buy me a drink."

"No," he said, "let's go right home. I'll follow you."

"Yes, sir!" I said sarcastically. You'd think I was working for him, instead of the other way around.

"When you pull into your driveway," he said, "don't get out of your car. Keep the engine running, crouch down in the seat, and make sure the doors are locked. Understand? I'll be right behind you, and we'll go in the house together."

"Why?" I asked, astounded.

"Because I said so," he replied firmly. "I don't tell you how to run your show; don't tell me how to do my job. Now just follow my instructions, got that?"

I stuck my tongue out at him.

When I got home, I did as he had told me, wondering if I were really in some kind of danger, and if so, how the hell would Chuck have known about it? Probably just being dramatic, I thought.

When we got into the house, he went straight to his little room, and I went into my beautifully furnished bedroom, got undressed and climbed into bed. I picked up the book that was lying open on the nighttable and began to read.

Soon, there was a knock at the bedroom door; a split second later Chuck was on top of me, totally nude, his strong, muscular black body against me. He made love to me in his wonderful, firm but gentle way.

CHAPTER 17

The next couple of months I spent seeing Mr. Big Shot at least three or four boring times a week. He took me to nice places, but so what? I could afford to take myself to nice places.

There were several important meetings I had to attend, with lawyers, accountants, Mr. Big Shot, Carolyn and her associate producers, and my agent. Soon the deal was set. I signed my name, and in a very short time I would have my own nighttime talk show.

The day the final contracts were signed, Mr. Big Shot took me to Chasen's for dinner.

"I'm so proud of you," he said with pathetic sincerity. "And I really love you, Claire. I love you very, very much." I believed he really meant it, too, and I felt kind of sorry for him. The love he felt for me I could never return.

A few days later, as I was puttering around the house, the doorbell rang. I looked out the window and saw an attractive, well-dressed, dark-haired woman of about 50 standing outside.

I opened the door. "Yes?" I asked.

"May I come in?" she asked. "I'm Rita Brown, Mrs. Jonathan Brown."

I stood there dumbly, taken completely by surprise.

This was Mr. Big Shot's wife, and she was certainly not dying.

She walked right past me into the living room.

"Sit down," I said, "can I get you something to drink?"

"No, thank you," she replied. "I'd like to make this visit brief. I came here from New York yesterday, and my plane back leaves in a couple of hours. I know you are having an affair with my husband, Ms. Stevens. That is what I've come to discuss with you."

I had a sinking feeling in the pit of my stomach.

"Mrs. Brown," I began, but she cut me off.

"What I would like to know, Ms. Stevens, is whether you are in love with him." Her voice trembled with emotion, and it tore at me.

"No, Mrs. Brown, I certainly am not."

She looked relieved, yet disgusted. She had probably never gone to bed with anyone she was not in love with, at least that was what her expression told me.

"And furthermore," I said, "I want you to understand that I didn't know . . ."

"You didn't know he was married," she said in a sing-song voice.

"Yes, I did!" I yelled. "I knew he was married! But I didn't know he was married to anyone like you!"

She looked at me as though I were crazy. She had probably seen my show, when I was in all my well-poised, charming glory. She probably had trouble believing that this half-inarticulate, emotional woman standing before her was really Claire Stevens. I'm surprised she didn't go outside and check the address to make sure she wasn't in the wrong house.

"And just what the hell is that supposed to mean?" she asked icily. "If you think I'm foolish for coming here . . ."

"No!" I shouted. "I don't think you're foolish! I'm the one who's a fool, the biggest God-damned fool in the world!" I burst into tears.

She sat there staring at me.

I grabbed her arm and she pulled it away, almost fearfully. She must have thought I was a mad-woman.

"Mrs. Brown, you've got to believe me!" Scenes of arguments between my mother and father because of his chasing around flashed through my mind. "I was told that you were in a sanitarium on Long Island, dying of a long-term illness . . ." It sounded ridiculous, even to me, as I said it.

She shook her head in disbelief. "He told you that? That I was dying?"

"No, no, no! Carolyn Barr told me that!"

"I don't know what in the hell you're talking about, young lady," Rita Brown said, rising, "but I'll tell you something. My husband has never been faithful to me, not in twenty-five years of marriage. I pretend not to notice, I put up with it, because I love him very much. I know that might be hard for someone like you to understand, but it's true. I have never done anything as degrading as this." Now her voice was beginning to break.

"Degrading?" I said. "What do you mean?"

"Coming here and talking to one of his . . . lovers," she said with disgust. "You see, the other girls never meant anything to him; I knew that and so I never pursued any of them about their affairs with my husband. But you, as much as I hate to say it, he's — he's in love with you, Miss Stevens. And I'm asking you, begging you, not to see him anymore. He'll get over you. Don't see him anymore, do you understand? Because if he ever left me, I don't know what I'd do." Suddenly her face contorted with rage. "If you ruin my marriage, I'll kill you," she shrieked. "I'll murder you, you Goddamn little bitch!" She collapsed on the sofa, sobbing uncontrollably.

I went to her and knelt down beside her. Tears were streaming down my face. "I promise you, Mrs. Brown, I'll never see him again. I mean that with all my heart. I'm sorry . . . so very, very sorry . . ."

She began to calm down, and when she looked at me, I think she believed me. She collected herself and walked out the door, without a word.

The door to Chuck's room, off to the side of the living room, opened.

"Whoo-ee!" he exclaimed. "Sounded like a soap opera!"

"Very funny," I replied coldly.

"Hey, come on, lighten up, Mary Clarissa. It wasn't your fault."

"Don't you call me that, you musclehead," I snapped. "To you, my name is Claire. I'm your boss, remember?"

"Hey, babe," he said threateningly, "don't take it out on me."

"What are you going to do, beat me up?!" I said sarcastically. I began to cry. "I'm so fed up with the people in my world. William," I mumbled, "William."

"Hey," he said, "take it easy, babe. I'd never hurt you. I'm very gentle with women; you should know that by now. Anyone who'd hit a woman is nothing but a punk coward."

I sighed. "Chuck," I said softly, "why don't you go back to whatever you were doing in your room? I need to be alone right now."

"Sure," he said softly. "I understand, Claire."

I smiled slightly. "Mary Clarissa's fine," I told him as he went back to his room and closed the door.

A few minutes later, the doorbell rang. Now what does she want from me, I thought, getting upset all over again.

I opened the door, expecting to see Rita Brown, and the next thing I knew I was flying across the room. It was Jim, and he was very drunk, a violent expression in his glazed eyes.

"You damned bitch," he snarled, "screwing around with that poor woman's husband! I'm the one who sent her here, you know."

I got up off the floor, my arm throbbing where I'd slammed it against the wall.

"Screwing around with another broad is one thing, but this is too much!"

I was careful not to look toward Chuck's door. He was waiting until Jim walked farther into the room so he could rush out and grab him, I figured. I didn't want to alert Jim to the fact that someone else was in the house.

"Jim" I said, "it wasn't what you're thinking. Besides, I'm not going to see him again. Now come in and sit down. You've got to calm down."

In a flash, his hand was in his pocket and out it came with a gun, pointed right at me.

Oh, my God, I thought, If Chuck comes out now, he's a dead man.

"You're coming back to me, bitch. And I mean right now. Otherwise I'll kill you!" he raged on.

"Please," I said, moving toward the sofa, hoping he would turn with me so that his back would be to Chuck's door. "Please, Jim!" I spoke loud enough to be sure Chuck could hear what I was saying. "Put the *gun* away. You know how afraid I am of *guns!*"

Without looking at it directly, I could see Chuck's door begin to open. Jim's back was now toward the door.

I kept talking so that if there were any noise made by the door opening, Jim wouldn't hear it.

"Please, Jim" I said in a loud voice, "put the gun away. I'll go back with you, if you still want me; I didn't think you still wanted me." Chuck was coming slowly out of the room. "I know you love me, and it's important to me, but you never tried to get in touch with me, and I thought you had somebody else."

Chuck sprang like a rattlesnake; at the same moment Jim turned and the gun went off, making a small hole in the wall. I was terrified. I screamed at the top of my lungs.

"Bastard!" Jim yelled. "Son of a bitch, I'll kill you!"

Chuck was bigger and stronger, but Jim's rage gave him additional strength. All I remember is screaming and screaming, standing there, not even having the sense to try to help, or duck down. I was frozen with fear, and the thumping I thought I heard in the background was my heart pounding, pumping adrenalin through my body.

They struggled, it seemed like forever, but probably was no more than a minute. Then I heard the popping sound of the gun going off again, and everything stopped. Jim fell backward, straight back like a wooden lump, landing on the floor in a grotesque position, where he lay motionless.

Chuck bent over him immediately, and felt for a pulse. I rushed over. The sight of him lying there made me sick to my stomach. His eyes were open, staring straight ahead, expressionless. Blood was seeping from under his shirt.

Chuck shook his head. "No pulse, no nothing," he said. "Hell, if only I hadn't been cleaning my own gun, I could have disarmed him easily and this might not have happened. Now, he's a gonner . . ."

"You don't know that," I told him. "I'm going to call an ambulance . . . and the police . . ."

He got up quickly and stepped in front of me. "I'll do it," he said. "You stay with him; watch for signs of life. But whatever you do, don't touch anything, especially not the gun."

I looked at the ugly black weapon; it made my skin crawl. It was the last thing in the world I wanted to touch.

He dialed the phone and spoke for a while. It didn't sound like he was talking to the police or calling an ambulance, but I was too upset to realize this fully or to care. I kept looking at Jim, knowing that in all probability he was stone dead. The blood looked like it was coming from where I thought his heart would be. The bullet must have gone right through.

"It was an accident," I said over and over, "an accident." My whole body was trembling, and I had trouble catching my breath.

Soon, I don't know how long after, probably only ten minutes or so, I became aware of sirens coming up the hill. They wow'ed to a stop in front of the house.

Paramedics came in, then went back out to the ambulance and came back with equipment. They worked over Jim, and were still trying to revive him when the police arrived.

"What happened here?" an officer asked, and Chuck stood with them, explaining what had happened while I sat frozen in a chair, staring straight ahead, feeling almost as dead as the body lying there on the floor.

Some more men arrived, police photographers, then other men came and covered Jim's body. They carried it out, and there were no sirens as they drove away. It probably was the coroner's office. No need to rush, not anymore.

The police told us we'd have to come down to the police station and make a statement.

"Do you feel all right, ma'am?" one of the officers asked kindly.

"Yes," I answered.

I went to my closet and got a sweater. I was freezing.

At the police station I answered their questions as though I were in a trance. Nothing seemed real to me. They questioned us separately, then in a room together. It seemed they were asking the same questions over and over, but I'm not sure. I was someplace else. I was in William's small, shabby apartment in Silver Lake, years ago; everything that had happened since was a dream.

I heard Chuck's voice answering the officers' questions, and it sounded far away. Then the police must have told us to leave, because Chuck was helping me up and soon we were out in the street, then in his car.

"I guess they believed what we told them," he said. "They want us to stay where we can be reached for more questioning, if it becomes necessary, though."

"Why shouldn't they believe us?" I asked innocently. "We told them the truth. It was an accident."

"Of course," he said, chuckling nervously, "but that doesn't mean they have to believe it."

I didn't answer; I couldn't think of anything to say. I didn't even realize we were on the way to Carolyn Barr's until Chuck pulled into her driveway.

She met us at the door.

"Come in, come in, Chuck," she said, then embraced me. "You poor thing. God, you look terrible. You're probably in shock. I'll have Cindy fix you a drink. All of us, in fact."

Cindy was the redhead I had seen there the first time I had dinner at Carolyn's home.

I sat down in an armchair, while Chuck and Carolyn sat on the sofa, talking. Suddenly, I realized that something was happening that I didn't understand.

"Wait a minute," I interrupted their conversation.

They both stopped talking and looked at me.

"Carolyn," I began slowly, "how did you know what happened? And you two seem to know each other..."

They both exchanged a glance. Carolyn looked questioningly at Chuck; he shrugged his shoulders.

Carolyn sighed. "I guess we might as well fill her in," she said quietly.

"Fill me in on what?" I asked listlessly. I didn't have enough energy left to feel any concern, or even much curiosity.

"Chuck works for me," Carolyn began. "I had hired him to watch you. When he saw you take off in your car that night you went to the singles bar, he followed you."

I smiled slightly. "What if I had decided to leave with someone else?"

"He would have thought of some way of stopping you," Carolyn said. "He's very resourceful."

At this, Chuck laughed heartily. "Thanks, babe!"

"That's why I pay him $1500 a week. He's got brains as well as brawn."

"Plus my $500, that's two thousand dollars a week. Pretty big money. Almost as much as I'm making, and I'm a star." I began to laugh hysterically. William, I thought, William, wake me up out of this nightmare.

"I'll reimburse you what you've paid him," Carolyn said, coming over and putting her arm on my shoulder. "Now try to calm down, hon. Drink your drink."

I didn't have the strength to argue with her. I picked up the drink and sipped it slowly. The one thing I didn't want to do in the middle of this bad dream was throw up. I don't know why, but that was what went through my mind.

"You'll reimburse me," I said, becoming hysterical, "You'll reimburse me!" I shoved Carolyn away from me. "A man is lying cold dead in the morgue, and you'll reimburse me!" I jumped up and threw over the small table next to where I had been sitting. The lamp crashed to the floor, and somehow I felt better.

Chuck was over in a flash, pushing me back into the chair, restraining me.

"Now look here, Marh Clarissa," he said firmly. "It was an accident. If I hadn't been there, he might have murdered you, and it would not have been an accident! Would that have been better?"

I started to cry.

Carolyn went and got a cool, wet towel and patted my face with it.

"Working for you, or pretending to, as it were, was his idea, not mine. Jim Robinson was beginning to act up." Carolyn said.

"He was acting up because you talked me into having an affair with that jerk network guy," I said in a monotone.

"No," Carolyn said. "Before that. His weak ego just couldn't stand your leaving him. The idea that it was not so bad because he thought you and I were together, was beginning to wear off. He called me every day, bugged me to let you go, and I kept stalling him. I didn't know how much longer he could last before he would pull something, like he did today."

"What if I hadn't gone to the singles bar that night?" I asked.

"Chuck had already come up with the idea of being your personal body guard," Carolyn explained. "In a few days, I was going to tell you that I thought you needed one, and I was going to recommend him."

"She had only your welfare at heart," the shy redhead piped up. It was the first full sentence I had heard her utter, including the first time I met her.

"Sure," I said despondently, "sure." I wasn't angry with Carolyn or Chuck, or anyone in particular, just at the whole lousy situation, my whole miserable life.

Carolyn put her hand on my arm. "And I'm sorry about lying to you about Jonathan Brown's wife," she said. "But I felt it had to be done. He has a reputation for running around anyway."

"I know," I said, my head beginning to throb. "The only thing that upset his wife was that he happened to fall in love with me. Everything ties up into a neat, pretty package; nobody did anything wrong; everybody winds up getting what he wants."

"Oh, stop moralizing," Carolyn said with annoyance. "You're not so innocent yourself, you know. You took my word for it about Brown's wife dying in a sanitarium. Did you bother to check my story? Obviously not. Don't tell me you weren't tempted by that nighttime talk show deal."

I laughed derisively. "Isn't it ironic that we probably won't get it after all? Brown will cancel the whole thing because I'm not going to see him again. And once what happened today hits the news, the network will cancel my show altogether, for sure."

"Is that what you want?" Carolyn said sharply. "Is it? Mama's good girl feels guilty, and wants to pay for her misdeeds? I'll tell you one thing I learned the hard way, babe. There's no such thing as retribution. It has no value. If you do something you think was wrong, admit it and don't do it again in the future. Sacrificing and punishing yourself doesn't change what you did one damned bit, nor does it remove any pain you may have caused someone else. The sooner you learn that, the better off you'll be, and so will everyone around you."

I listened to what she said. You couldn't help but listen to Carolyn. It made plenty of sense, but still I fought it.

"Maybe I just wasn't cut out to be a star," I said softly.

"Ah, good old self pity. Another way of assuaging the troubled conscience. 'Look at poor little me, see how I'm making myself suffer down here on the ground. Haven't I suffered enough yet? Won't someone please pick me up off the ground so I can be a good girl once more.' The only one who decided whether you were 'cut out' to be a star, was you!"

"She's right, babe, you know," Chuck agreed. "Like that guy, William, who you're obviously still in love with. You're the one who walked out on him; that's what you told me, isn't it?"

I nodded sullenly.

"Well, why the hell have you never gone back to him and told *him* how sorry you were, instead of torturing yourself? The worst he can do is say forget it, and then you won't be any worse off than you were in the first place."

I resented their lecturing, but it was beginning to take effect.

"And another thing I can't understand about you show biz people," Chuck continued, "is why so many of you feel you can't have a successful career and love in your life as well. It makes absolutely no sense. Bodyguards do it. Accountants do it. Veterinarians do it. Why are entertainers so damned special that you can't combine work with love?"

I didn't have much of an answer. "I don't know why," I said. "It just seems to work out that way."

"Nothing just works out any particular way," Carolyn said. "Most of the time, barring accidents and Acts of God, we make things work out the way they do."

"Even if William would take me back, which I doubt," I told them, "he'd never be able to tolerate my being the breadwinner. He's a gifted actor, much more talented than me."

"Oh, really?" said Carolyn. "That's the first I'm hearing about this. If he's so good, maybe I'd like to meet him. The industry can always use gifted actors."

"I never thought of any of this," I mumbled, amazed. "I never thought of doing any of the things you're saying."

"That's what's so destructive about living with guilt," Carolyn said. "It paralyzes you, makes you work against yourself and everyone around you, even on an unconscious level. You program yourself for total defeat, or partial defeat, depending on the amount of guilt you carry with you. And by the way," she added, smiling, "the accident today will in no way affect our show. You'll see."

"But the papers will say that your former personal manager had been threatening you and your producer — that's me, in case you forgot — and so you hired a bodyguard to protect you. Today, he did his job, protecting you from that drunken, violent maniac who was threatening you with a loaded gun. They struggled, and Jim got shot. If it was anyone's fault, it was his own."

"Well, of course, I agreed. "I saw it with my own eyes. It's just that the whole thing is so sad."

"Not nearly as sad as it would have been if *I* had been in front of that damn gun when it went off," Chuck laughed.

I got up and went over to him. I touched his hand. "You saved my life today, Chuck," I said quietly. "And I'm very, very grateful to you."

"Ah, shucks," he teased, "t'was nuthin', ma'am!"

But it was just the opposite — it was everything. And what they said to me started me thinking. It took time, of course, but gradually I began to operate on a new premise — guilt was destructive, the past was past and couldn't be changed. Without even trying, I began to live more constructively. I made plans for the future, but only tentative ones. No one knew, after all, what the future would bring. I concentrated on living in the present, day by day, and I felt lighter and happier than I ever had. Even my work improved; Carolyn noticed the difference, too. I could tell my guests were responding to me even more.

I came to accept the fact that my mother was dead, and that she would never know that I had changed my whole life to suit the ambitions she'd had for me when she was alive. I sat down and considered if I was really doing what I wanted to do with my life. The answer, I realized, was yes. I loved my work, enjoyed every minute of it. Had I stayed with straight acting, the answer might have been no, because I didn't really enjoy acting. But I loved doing my talk show, and I got a lot more out of it than money and fame. I got real satisfaction from my work. The only thing missing was William.

CHAPTER 18

Carolyn had been accurate in her prediction. The newspapers ran the story of the accident, and it quickly blew over. There was, of course, the usual gossip, but we received very little flack from the network people.

I never got the chance to turn down Mr. Big Shot, because I never heard from him again. A new set was built for my nighttime, prime time talk show, and rehearsals began. I was as excited as I could be. This was really big time.

I wanted so much to get back together with William. I kept picturing in my mind how wonderful it would be, to see him again, go out with him, sleep with him, marry him. I realized there was only one person who could start the ball rolling if any of my dreams were to come true concerning William. That person was obviously me.

One day, after I left the studio, I felt confident enough to do what I had been planning. I drove to Silver Lake, to the place where I hoped William still lived.

I started to get cold feet when I saw a light on in the window, but I made myself get out of the car. The name on the mailbox jumped out at me: WILLIAM JONES. So he still lived there, after all this time.

I stood outside the door for a while, trying to work up enough nerve to knock at the door. He would open it, and

I would be face to face with the one man I loved. But what would his reaction be?

I walked back to my car, and almost got in. Damn, I thought, I'm here, I'm going to do it! I wanted so much to see him, touch him.

I went back to the door. I ran my hand along the wood. All that stood between me and William was that thin piece of wood. Finally, I forced myself to knock.

"Yeah?" I heard William's voice from inside. "Who is it?" He opened the door.

He just stood there, for a split second, his face registering no expression while his mind grasped the situation. Then the surprise began to show.

"Aren't you going to ask me in?" I asked softly.

"Sure," he said, stepping out of the way.

I walked in. For want of something to say, I looked around the room.

"It's so good to be here again," I said. "And you got a new chair." I remember I said that, believe it or not. I walked over and sat down. "It's comfortable," I told him. "Looks nice too."

"Yeah," he answered. "The guy next door moved and he gave it to me."

"You mean the dude who used to have all the wild parties?"

"Yeah," he answered, and I could see he was remembering all the times he had called the guy when he woke us up in the middle of the night. The man worked until 1 a.m. in a factory someplace; his parties would start about two in the morning.

"Why'd he move?" I laughed, relieving my tension. "Was he finally evicted?"

William laughed too. "I don't know. Probably was. He used to wake up the whole neighborhood."

We looked at each other then, really looked at each other for the first time since my surprise arrival.

"Mary Clarissa," he said walking over to me. "What are you doing here? I mean, I just don't believe it, man, I just don't believe it." He touched my arm, almost as if to make sure I was real.

"Neither do I, William. I just . . ." I couldn't say any more. No words would come forth, and I tried to hold back my tears. "I'm . . . I'm just so happy to see you . . ." I couldn't control myself any longer.

"Hey, baby, there's nothing to cry about. I'm happy to see you too." He took me in his arms and rocked me gently back and forth.

"Come on," he said, "let's have a drink." He went to the refrigerator and took out a bottle of white wine. "I hope this is okay," he said. "I wasn't expecting company."

"It's fine, William, perfect," I told him.

He sat down on the sofa with his glass of wine. "So what do we say now?"

"I have so much to say, William. Only none of it will come out."

"I thought of you so much, so often," he said. "You look wonderful."

I wanted to go over to him, throw myself into his arms, but I was afraid.

He looked at me, and there was wonder in his eyes. "You still love me, don't you, Mary Clarissa?"

"Oh, yes, William, yes. Please hold me," I cried.

He walked over, lifted me out of the chair and carried me into the bedroom. I just kept my arms around his neck, holding him tight, never wanting to let him go.

He laid me down on the bed, gently, tenderly, then kissed me and started to undress me. He kissed every part of my body, and when we made love at first he was slow and gentle, then he went wild with passion. I responded to all of it, every minute, every second, until the glorious moment when we came together.

We slept together, wrapped in each other's arms. I had

the most wonderful dreams, and when I woke up, the first rays of sunlight wree appearing through the sheer window curtains.

I looked over; William was already up, and I heard sounds coming from the kitchen, pleasant morning sounds of water running in the sink, coffee percolating on the gas stove.

I went into the bathroom, washed my face, threw on William's robe which was hanging on a large hook attached to the bathroom door.

"Good morning," I said brightly, walking into the kitchen.

He already had two mugs of strong coffee on the table. He made the best coffee.

His eyes brightened when he turned and saw me. Then I noticed the trace of a frown. My heart started to sink.

"Sit down," he said, "let's have our coffee. We have to talk, Mary Clarissa." His face was drawn and he had the familiar intense expression.

"Sure, babe," I said, my voice trembling. "Fire away."

"I've been up all night, Mary Clarissa, thinking, thinking, thinking. And I came up empty. You were prepared for this reunion; I wasn't. My feelings are running helter skelter; I don't know which end is up."

"Do you still love me?" I felt he did, but . . .

"I don't know, Mary Clarissa, I just don't know."

I must have looked stricken.

He touched my face. "It's too sudden, hon. Just give me a little time. Don't give up on me. Just give me a little time. One thing I know, I could never again go through another breakup. I'd crack, man, I'd just crack up."

"All right," I agreed reluctantly. "I guess I owe you that much at least, huh?"

"Don't put it that way," he said sharply. "If it turns out we can't make it together anymore, it'll be both our faults, not just yours."

"Goodbye," I said, then rushed into the bedroom, got dressed, and left quickly without saying another word. I tried not to look at him, but I could see him standing there, confused and helpless. I got into my car, started it up, and drove away.

There were two weeks left until the taping of our first night show, and there were kinks that had to be worked out. I tried my best to keep my mind on my work, but every time I was paged on the set, my heart leaped in hopes that it was William calling. When I left the studio each night, I couldn't help looking around the parking lot, hoping to see him standing there waiting for me, waiting to tell me he still loved me and wanted me to come back. But as the days went slowly by and nothing happened, I began to lose hope. If the answer is no, I'll just have to accept his decision, I thought, the way he had accepted mine so long ago.

Then the big day arrived. We would be taping the crucial opening night show, and I forced myself to concentrate, psyched myself into putting every ounce of my energy into my work. It wasn't only for myself that I had to succeed, but for Carolyn and everyone who had backed me. Careers were at stake; big money was involved. We would be picking up a whole new audience all over the country, and the show had to be more than good, it had to be exceptional, or heads would roll, including ine.

"Quiet on the set!" the assistant director yelled. "Quiet on the set!" And suddenly there was silence. Just before the red light came on the camera, signifying that the tape was rolling, I always looked out at my studio audience, smiled at them, and blew them a kiss. Without my audience, where would I be? Now, I looked out at them and my mouth dropped open. There was William, sitting in the front row, grinning and making the "okay" sign with his hand.

The red light came on. "Rolling," the sound man called out. The assistant director, having received the "cue talent" command through his earphone from the director in the control room, held up both hands, fingers spread. "Ten seconds . . ."

I faced the camera, smiling and fighting to hold back my tears of joy.

"Ladies and gentlemen," the announcer intoned, "*Claire Stevens!*" Applause from the audience, and we were off and running.

After the taping, William and I drove straight to Las Vegas and got married that same night.

"You know how I got into that studio?" he told me, laughing. "I paid fifty dollars cash to some tourist on the line, for his free ticket!"

"Well, that's true love, William!" I teased him. I was so happy to be his wife.

"I love you very, very much, Mary Clarissa," he said seriously, and took me in his arms.

When we got back to L.A., I brought William over to meet Carolyn. He read for her and did one of his audition monologues. She was very impressed.

"You, young man, are a terrific actor," she said, and I knew she meant it.

She introduced him to a good agent, and within two weeks, he was getting day parts on the series, both drama and sit-com.

"Finally," William said, "finally I'm working as an actor in this town!"

Every time he got cast, we would celebrate with wine, crackers and cheese, just like in the old days.

Soon he got a part in a film, a week's work in a small but heavy role. The director was astounded by William's excellent acting ability.

We rented out my house in Laurel Canyon and leased a small, cozy home in the Hollywood Hills, near the famous "Hollywood" sign. Each day, we come closer to one another, and love each other more.

I'm still doing my night time talk show, and while I'm not the female Johnny Carson yet, I'm holding my own in the ratings, and enjoying every minute of it.

Just the other day, William came home with some exciting news.

"I got it!" he announced, and took me in his arms.

He had landed the main supporting role in a major film to be done at Universal Studios. Of course, we celebrated in our usual way, but more so!

"Your husband is a gold mine as an actor," Carolyn told me today on the phone. "All he needed was someone like me to discover him! And listen to this, Claire: I have a strong feeling he's going to be nominated for Best Supporting Actor for this role he just got. The film's a real biggie, and William's got what it takes!"

"Yes, Carolyn, but do you think he'll win?" I teased.

"I don't know that for sure, babe," she said seriously. "But I know he'll be nominated."

A big smile came over my face. You know Carolyn Barr — she's always right!

MELROSE SQUARE BLACK AMERICAN SERIES

These highly acclaimed quality format paperback editions are profusely illustrated, meticulously researched and fully indexed. $3.95 ea.

- ☐ **NAT TURNER:** Prophet and Slave Revolt Leader
- ☐ **PAUL ROBESON:** Athlete, Actor, Singer, Activist
- ☐ **ELLA FITZGERALD:** First Lady of American Song
- ☐ **MALCOLM X:** Militant Black Leader
- ☐ **JACKIE ROBINSON:** First Black in Professional Baseball
- ☐ **MATTHEW HENSON:** Arctic Explorer
- ☐ **SCOTT JOPLIN:** Composer
- ☐ **LOUIS ARMSTRONG:** Musician
- ☐ **SOJOURNER TRUTH:** Antislavery Activist
- ☐ **CHESTER HIMES:** Author and Civil Rights Pioneer
- ☐ **BILLIE HOLIDAY:** Singer
- ☐ **RICHARD WRIGHT:** Author
- ☐ **ALTHEA GIBSON:** Tennis Champion
- ☐ **JAMES BALDWIN:** Author
- ☐ **WILMA RUDOLPH:** Champion Athlete
- ☐ **SIDNEY POITIER:** Actor
- ☐ **JESSE OWENS:** Olympic Superstar
- ☐ **MARCUS GARVEY:** Black Nationalist Leader
- ☐ **JOE LOUIS:** Boxing Champion
- ☐ **HARRY BELAFONTE:** Singer & Actor
- ☐ **LENA HORNE:** Singer & Actor

HOLLOWAY HOUSE PUBLISHING CO.

8060 Melrose Ave., Los Angeles, California 90046

- ☐ **NAT TURNER** (ISBN 0-87067-551-6) $3.95
- ☐ **PAUL ROBESON** (ISBN 0-87067-552-4) $3.95
- ☐ **ELLA FITZGERALD** (ISBN 0-87067-553-2) $3.95
- ☐ **MALCOLM X** (ISBN 0-87067-554-0) $3.95
- ☐ **JACKIE ROBINSON** (ISBN 0-87067-555-9) $3.95
- ☐ **MATTHEW HENSON** (ISBN 0-87067-556-7) $3.95
- ☐ **SCOTT JOPLIN** (ISBN 0-87067-557-5) $3.95
- ☐ **LOUIS ARMSTRONG** (ISBN 0-87067-558-3) $3.95
- ☐ **SOJOURNER TRUTH** (ISBN 0-87067-559-1).... $3.95
- ☐ **CHESTER HIMES** (ISBN 0-87067-560-5) $3.95
- ☐ **BILLIE HOLIDAY** (ISBN 0-87067-561-3) $3.95
- ☐ **RICHARD WRIGHT** (ISBN 0-87067-562-1) $3.95
- ☐ **ALTHEA GIBSON** (ISBN 0-87067-563-X) $3.95
- ☐ **JAMES BALDWIN** (ISBN 0-87067-564-8) $3.95
- ☐ **WILMA RUDOLPH** (ISBN 0-87067-565-6) $3.95
- ☐ **SIDNEY POITIER** (ISBN 0-87067-566-4) $3.95
- ☐ **JESSE OWENS** (ISBN 0-87067-567-2) $3.95
- ☐ **MARCUS GARVEY** (ISBN 0-87067-568-0) $3.95
- ☐ **JOE LOUIS** (ISBN 0-87067-570-2) $3.95
- ☐ **HARRY BELAFONTE** (ISBN 0-87067-571-0) ... $3.95
- ☐ **LENA HORNE** (ISBN 0-87067-572-9) $3.95

Gentlemen I enclose $ _____ ☐ cash ☐ check ☐ money order, payment in full for books ordered. I understand that if I am not completely satisfied, I may return my order within 10 days for a complete refund. (Add $1.00 per order to cover postage and handling. CA Residents add 8¼% sales tax 15¢ per book. Please allow 6 weeks for delivery.)

Name _____

Address _____

City _____ State _____ Zip _____

PSEUDO COOL
BY JOSEPH E. GREEN

A Novel of today's black, wealthy and privileged youth

Five black seniors at a prestigious west coast university each have a secret: one sells herself to pay the expensive tuition; one drinks heavily and sleeps with white girls in an attempt to disinheit his blackness; another is gay, and living in the closet; another is a poor girl adopted into a high society family; two believe they were responsible for a friend's death. Each is thinking only of graduation. Each believes that the answer to the problems that plague them lies just the other side of college life

Pseudo Cool is a tough, shocking first novel in the genre of the sensational bestseller, Less Than Zero. Joseph E. Green is a student at Stanford University.

HOLLOWAY HOUSE PUBLISHING CO.
8060 MELROSE AVE., LOS ANGELES, CA 90046

Gentlemen: I enclose $_____ ☐ cash, ☐ check, ☐ money order, payment in full for books ordered. I understand that if I am not completely satisfied, I may return my order within 10 days for a complete refund. (Add .90 cents per order to cover postage. California residents add 6½% sales tax. Please allow four weeks for delivery. ☐ **BH 329-7 $2.95 Pseduo Cool**

Name _____
Address _____
City_____State_____Zip_____

TRIUMPH & TRAGEDY
The True Story of the
THE SUPREMES

By Marianne Ruuth

No Holds Barred!

Marianne Ruuth interviewed former members of The Supremes, friends and associates for an in-depth look at those three young women that all of American fell in love with back in the 1960s. They were: Florence Ballard ("the shy one"), Mary Wilson ("the one many considered to be the most talented") and Diana Ross ("the one determined to become a star"), all from Detroit and all terribly innocent in the beginning. Florence became the figure of tragedy: She died very young, living on welfare. Mary, still performing, found something of a normal life for a star... and we all know that Diana realized her ambition of becoming a Superstar. Now read the real story behind the headlines and the gossip!

HOLLOWAY HOUSE PUBLISHING CO.
8060 MELROSE AVE., LOS ANGELES, CA 90046

Gentlemen: I enclose $_____ ☐ cash, ☐ check, ☐ money order, payment in full for books ordered. I understand that if I am not completely satisfied, I may return my order within 10 days for a complete refund. (Add 75 cents per order to cover postage. California residents add 6½% sales tax. Please allow three weeks for delivery.)

■ **BH725-X TRIUMPH & TRAGEDY $2.95**

Name _____

Address _____

City _____ State _____ Zip _____

The Saga of Five Generations of

A MISSISSIPPI FAMILY

By Barbara Johnson
With Mary Sikora

A stirring tale of one family's rise from slavery to respect: From poverty to relative comfort, *A Mississippi Family* is, like *Roots* based on those things remembered—deaths, weddings, tragedy, tears and laughter—and passed on to generation after generation. Barbara Johnson, born and raised in central Mississippi where most of the story takes place, has done a remarkable job of turning oral history into a wonderful book. The Elams and many of their descendants are unforgettable characters, ones that you won't soon forget ...and will stir warm memories of your own.

HOLLOWAY HOUSE PUBLISHING CO.
8060 MELROSE AVE., LOS ANGELES, CA 90046

Gentlemen: I enclose $_____ ☐ cash, ☐ check, ☐ money order, payment in full for books ordered. I understand that if I am not completely satisfied, I may return my order within 10 days for a complete refund. (Add 75 cents per order to cover postage. California residents add 6½% sales tax. Please allow three weeks for delivery.)

☐ **BH272-X A MISSISSIPPI FAMILY $2.50**

Name _____

Address _____

City _____ State _____ Zip _____

RICHARD PRYOR
THE MAN BEHIND THE LAUGHTER

BIOGRAPHY—The most famous comedian in America today—and the most controversial—Richard Pryor's life story reads like a work of exciting, if improbable fiction. His self-confessed beginnings in Peoria, Illinois, where his mother was a prostitute in his grandmother's bordello; his life on the streets as a young man; his sturggle to break into show business on his own uncompromising terms; his acknowledged use of cocaine and other drugs; and his near brush with death after a mystery fire at his home in California have all provided material for his shocking comic portrayals. If the past is an indicator of the future, Pryor will continue to shock, titillate and make the world laugh with him for many years to come.

HOLLOWAY HOUSE PUBLISHING CO.
8060 MELROSE AVE., LOS ANGELES, CALIF. 90046

Gentlemen: I enclose _____ ☐ cash, ☐ check, ☐ money order, payment in full for books ordered. I understand that if I am not completely satisfied, I may return my order within 10 days for a complete refund. (Add 50c per order to cover postage. California residents add 6% tax. Please allow three weeks for delivery.)

☐ **BH013 RICHARD PRYOR $2.25**

Name _____

Address _____

City _____ State _____ Zip _____

Personal Sketches of Los Angeles

SECRET MUSIC

BY ODIE HAWKINS

Utilizing the same thrust, power, and formula that made his *Ghetto Sketches* his first bestseller, Odie Hawkins moves the focus from Chicago, where he grew up, to Los Angeles, where he has lived for the past twenty years. And, once again, he has peopled his story with unforgettable characters; there is the telephone freak who drastically changes the lives of several of his victims, bringing ruin to a young virgin, death to a housewife, and happiness to a lonely old woman. Here is a mixed bag of odd lots that only Hawkins could invent. Or does he invent them?

HOLLOWAY HOUSE PUBLISHING CO.
8060 MELROSE AVE., LOS ANGELES, CA 90046

Gentlemen: I enclose $_____ ☐ cash, ☐ check, ☐ money order, payment in full for books ordered. I understand that if I am not completely satisfied, I may return my order within 10 days for a complete refund. (Add 90 cents per book to cover postage. California residents add 6½% sales tax. Please allow three weeks for delivery.)

☐ BH265-7 **SECRET MUSIC.** $2.95

Name _____

Address _____

City _____ State _____ Zip _____

TO KILL A BLACK MAN

By Louis E. Lomax

A compelling dual biography of the two men who changed America's way of thinking—Malcolm X and Martin Luther King, Jr.

Louis E. Lomax was a close friend to both Malcolm X and Dr. Martin Luther King, Jr. In this dual biography, he includes much that Malcolm X did not tell in his autobiography and dissects Malcolm's famous letters. Lomax writes with the sympathy and understanding of a friend but he is also quick to point out the shortcomings of both Dr. King and Malcolm X—and what he believed was the reasons for their failure to achieve their goals and to obtain the full support of all their people. And he does not hesitate in pointing a finger at those he believes to be responsible for the deaths of his friends. "A valuable addition to the available information on the murders of Martin Luther King, Jr. and Malcolm X," says the *Litterair Passport*. Louis Lomax gained national prominence with such books as *The Black Revolt, When The Word Is Given*, and *To Kill A Black Man*. At the time of his death in an automobile accident he was a professor at Hofstra University.

HOLLOWAY HOUSE PUBLISHING CO.
8060 MELROSE AVE., LOS ANGELES, CALIF. 90046

Gentlemen: I enclose _____ ☐ cash, ☐ check, ☐ money order, payment in full for books ordered. I understand that if I am not completely satisfied, I may return my order within 10 days for a complete refund. (Add 75c per order to cover postage. California residents add 6½% tax. Please allow three weeks for delivery.)

☐ BH731-4 **TO KILL A BLACK MAN** $3.25

Name _____

Address _____

City _____ State _____ Zip _____

REUNION

By Mark Allen Boone

The Fascinating Story of One Man's Fight to Regain His Family's Honor...

Reunion is the story of two friends, and one man's determination to find his origin. Mostly, it's a story about friendship—the kind that goes way beyond family and blood; the kind that lives forever. Levi Merriweather and Wesley Luckett are such friends. They're the best of friends. They shared everything, even the same woman. But friends sometimes grow apart. And then something happens that brings them back together.

☐ BH 331-9   **REUNION** $2.95

HOLLOWAY HOUSE PUBLISHING CO.
8060 MELROSE AVE., LOS ANGELES, CA 90046

Gentlemen: I enclose $_____ ☐ cash, ☐ check, ☐ money order, payment in full for books ordered. I understand that if I am not completely satisfied, I may return my order within 10 days for a complete refund. (Add 75 cents per order to cover postage. California residents add 6½% sales tax. Please allow three weeks for delivery.)

Name _____

Address _____

City _____ State _____ Zip _____

SCARS AND MEMORIES: THE STORY OF A LIFE

By Odie Hawkins

Scars and Memories is Odie Hawkins' deeply personal story of his life's journey, from a childhood in Chicago where he was one of the "poorest of the poor" to highly paid Hollywood screenwriter with his own office—and those people, mostly women, who mattered to him along the way. *Scars and Memories* is a tough, gritty book about a survivor who, as a child, lived in dank, cold tenement basements where the cockroaches were so thick on the walls he could set fire to them with rolled up newpapers, where there was seldom enough food, where sex and drugs were as commonplace as summer rain and winter chill. This is a deeply personal story, sometimes painfully told, that only a writer of Hawkins maturity and skill could write. Odie Hawkins is the author of the novels *Chicago Hustle, Chili, The Busting Out of An Orindary Man, Ghetto Sketches* and *Sweet Peter Deeder*

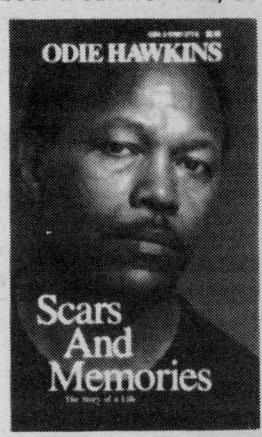

HOLLOWAY HOUSE PUBLISHING CO.
8060 MELROSE AVE., LOS ANGELES, CA 90046

Gentlemen: I enclose $_____ ☐ cash, ☐ check, ☐ money order, payment in full for books ordered. I understand that if I am not completely satisfied, I may return my order within 10 days for a complete refund. (Add 75 cents per order to cover postage. California residents add 6½% sales tax. Please allow three weeks for delivery.) ☐ **BH277-0 SCARS AND MEMORIES, $2.50**

Name _____

Address _____

City _____ State _____ Zip _____

JESSE JACKSON

By Eddie Stone

An Intimate Portrait of the Most Charismatic Man in American Politics

He's dynamic, charming, intelligent and has more charisma than any man to rocket into the American political arena since John F. Kennedy. One of the country's most popular black leaders, he is not without his critics. To many he is just too flamboyant, others find his political ideas somewhat vague, still others call him a blatant opportunist. Nevertheless he has proven he can pull in the votes whether it's in Vermont, or Mississippi, or Michigan. Jackson will play a major—and far reaching—role in American politics in the years to come.

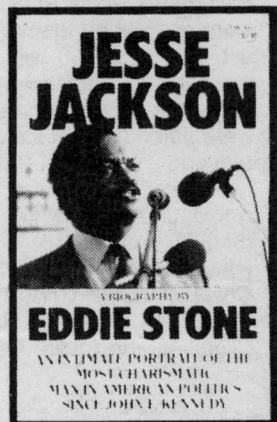

HOLLOWAY HOUSE PUBLISHING CO.
8060 MELROSE AVE., LOS ANGELES, CA 90046

Gentlemen: I enclose $_____ ☐ cash, ☐ check, ☐ money order, payment in full for books ordered. I understand that if I am not completely satisfied, I may return my order within 10 days for a complete refund. (Add 90 cents per book to cover postage. California residents add 6½% sales tax. Please allow three weeks for delivery.) **840-X JESSE JACKSON $3.95**

Name _____

Address _____

City _____ State _____ Zip _____

DIVA

BY STANLEY BENNETT CLAY

Terror Stalks the Glitzy World of a Famous Black Superstar!

Beautiful, talented Ida Lake was known as "The Diva" to her millions of fans when she reigned as Hollywood's black singing sensation of the '40s. Her career—and her sanity—collapsed after the suspicious deaths of the husband she adored and the daughter she worshipped and, haunted by rumors of "un-American" activities, Ida took refuge abroad. Two decades later, she has been coaxed into a comeback as the star of a Broadway musical. But tragedy stalks Ida Lake once again as a mysterious web of intrigue, sex scandal and murder envelops the show.

In *Diva*, author Stanley Bennett Clay captures the glamour—and suspense—that is show business.

HOLLOWAY HOUSE PUBLISHING CO.
8060 MELROSE AVE., LOS ANGELES, CA 90046

Gentlemen: I enclose $_____ ☐ cash, ☐ check, ☐ money order, payment in full for books ordered. I understand that if I am not completely satisfied, I may return my order within 10 days for a complete refund. (Add 90 cents per book to cover postage. California residents add 6½% sales tax. Please allow three weeks for delivery.) **839-6 DIVA $3.50**

Name _____

Address _____

City _____ State _____ Zip _____

BORDERLINE
The Case Of Too Many Graves
By W.J. Amos

Once again, William Amos, the author of M.I.A. Saigon, delivers a hard-hitting story of a man teased—and trapped— by circumstances beyond his control!

The jungles of 'Nam were a piece of cake compared to the deadly drama Cal Robbins gets himself caught up in back home. His accidental discovery of buried treasure in New Mexico unleashes a nightmare of mistaken identity, murder and mayhem. There's just no peace for the living ... when you're always on the borderline.

HOLLOWAY HOUSE PUBLISHING CO.
8060 MELROSE AVE., LOS ANGELES, CA 90046

Gentlemen: I enclose $_____ ☐ cash, ☐ check, ☐ money order, payment in full for books ordered. I understand that if I am not completely satisfied, I may return my order within 10 days for a complete refund. (Add 75 cents per order to cover postage. California residents add 6½% sales tax. Please allow three weeks for delivery.) ☐ **BH351 BORDERLINE $2.95**

Name _____
Address _____
City_____ State_____ Zip_____

INSIDE THE GREEN CIRCLE

By Glen T. Brock

It's the Last Place You Want To Find Yourself!

There was a maniac loose in Atlanta's parks, stalking unsuspecting couples who parked on the night lanes to talk, make out, make love. Their presence offended him, his sense of propriety, his sense of what was right. It was his duty to cleanse the world of fornicators. He was the avenging hand of God and they were the ejaculate of Satan. He was the hunter and they were the hunted.

But there was another hunter in the park, hired by a man who believed in circumventing the law. A man who'd appointed himself judge, jury and executioner. His prey was anyone who found themselves inside the green circle of his gun sight. And with him on the loose the cops became, like all the others, the hunters and the hunted!

HOLLOWAY HOUSE PUBLISHING CO.
8060 MELROSE AVE., LOS ANGELES, CA 90046

Gentlemen: I enclose $_____ ☐ cash, ☐ check, ☐ money order, payment in full for books ordered. I understand that if I am not completely satisfied, I may return my order within 10 days for a complete refund. (Add 75 cents per order to cover postage. California residents add 6½% sales tax. Please allow three weeks for delivery.)

☐ **BH299-1 INSIDE THE GREEN CIRCLE** $2.50

Name _____

Address _____

City _____ State _____ Zip _____

CANNIBALS
By Thurman Hoskins

A compelling tale of yesterday's homeless—hobos. Men, women, black, white; their will to live was a celebration of the human spirit. In the hobo jungles of the 1920's no act was considered too perverted. It was a world where the bigger fish ate the smaller, where the meanest wolf won the fight, and where the most cunning, cruel, and monstrous hobos ruled the jungle. It was a terrible place to be if you were black, unthinkable if you were black and a woman. But there were women, and children, black and white. They were all victims.

And in the Missouri railroad crossroads town of Waldron, there was even a worse force to contend with: The Ku Klux Klan.

HOLLOWAY HOUSE PUBLISHING CO.
8060 MELROSE AVE., LOS ANGELES, CA 90046

Gentlemen: I enclose $_____ ☐ cash, ☐ check, ☐ money order, payment in full for books ordered. I understand that if I am not completely satisfied, I may return my order within 10 days for a complete refund. (Add 75 cents per order to cover postage. California residents add 6½% sales tax. Please allow three weeks for delivery.) ☐ **BH350 CANNIBALS $2.95**

Name _____
Address _____
City _____ State _____ Zip _____

EDDIE
By Marianne Ruuth

24 PAGES OF PHOTOGRAPHS

THE BIOGRAPHY OF THE YEAR. LIVELY, BRILLIANT, INSIGHTFUL!

". . . the most dynamic new comic talent around," says *Newsweek*.

". . . swift as a shark," says film critic Pauline Kael.

". . . a genius . . . the Muhammad Ali of comedy," say his co-workers.

BEYOND BRILLIANCE

His *Beverly Hills Cop* director, Martin Brest, coined a phrase for Eddie Murphy . . . "beyond brilliance." He is a star of super magnitude, a super nova exploding to dazzle the world and Marianne Ruuth has captured this magic in a book as fascinating and dazzling as its subject.

24 PAGES OF PHOTOGRAPHS
EDDIE MURPHY'S PERSONAL HOROSCOPE

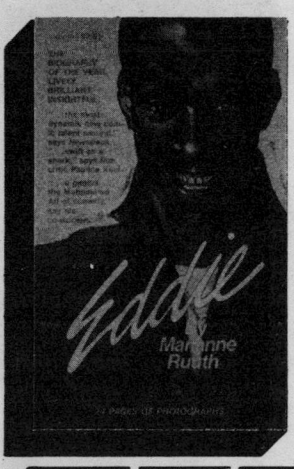

HOLLOWAY HOUSE PUBLISHING CO.
8060 MELROSE AVE., LOS ANGELES, CA 90046

Gentlemen: I enclose $_____ ☐ cash, ☐ check, ☐ money order, payment in full for books ordered. I understand that if I am not completely satisfied, I may return my order within 10 days for a complete refund. (Add 75 cents per order to cover postage. California residents add 6½% sales tax. Please allow three weeks for delivery.)

☐ BH717-9 **EDDIE** $2.95

Name _____
Address _____
City _____ State _____ Zip _____

THE DOWRY

By Ginger Whitaker

Few Things Come Without A Price. Love Is One Of Them.

Carrie Brown was young and beautiful, and a mystery the townspeople couldn't figure out. Left motherless at birth, she was sheltered her whole life by an over-protective and bitter father, the deacon of the Deliverance Church. The townspeople observed her from a distance, never really knowing her, only knowing about her. One person, Jimmy McCormack, paid particular attention to Carrie. For Jimmy, she was the answer to the age old gnawing in his heart. He would do anything to have Carrie Brown. Anything. Even buy her. But what Jimmy ends up paying and what Carrie ends up getting, are not what either had expected.

☐ BH 332-7   **THE DOWRY** $3.50

HOLLOWAY HOUSE PUBLISHING CO.
8060 MELROSE AVE., LOS ANGELES, CA 90048

Gentlemen: I enclose $_____ ☐ cash, ☐ check, ☐ money order, payment in full for books ordered. I understand that if I am not completely satisfied, I may return my order within 10 days for a complete refund. (Add 75 cents per order to cover postage. California residents add 6½% sales tax. Please allow three weeks for delivery.)

Name _____
Address _____
City _____ **State** _____ **Zip** _____

RIP & RUN
By Thurman Hoskins

Calvin and Holly Wanted to Live Like Bad, Bad Street Dudes. Problem Was, They Couldn't Do Anything, Anything, Right.

They wanted to become the Vice Lords of Ohio. However, Ohio already had several of those. Their own neighborhood had one, Robert Earl. Now old. R.E. wasn't the smartest man that ever lived but he wasn't all that dumb, either. He'd moved from an Alabama cotton field up to penthouse living and he was not about to let two punks like Holly and Calvin cut in on a dime of his take. Certainly not those two. They couldn't even rob a redneck cowboy's van without getting caught red handed. Their attention span was about zero except when it came to women. Any woman. Ugly women could distract them from the business at hand, that usually being trying to rob somebody or to juice Robert Earl. Talk about dump . . . but you won't forget them because. . . *Rip & Run* is a very funny book.

HOLLOWAY HOUSE PUBLISHING CO.
8060 MELROSE AVE., LOS ANGELES, CA 90046

Gentlemen: I enclose $_____ ☐ cash, ☐ check, ☐ money order, payment in full for books ordered. I understand that if I am not completely satisfied, I may return my order within 10 days for a complete refund. (Add .90 cents per order to cover postage. California residents add 6½% sales tax. Please allow four weeks for delivery. ☐ **BH 200-2 $2.95 Rip & Run**

Name _____
Address _____
City _____ State _____ Zip _____

MEMPHIS BLUES

BY BRETT HOWARD

In a wonderfully romantic weave of fact and fiction, Brett Howard tells the story of Harold Green, an orphan dumped on the Memphis Beale Street river landing in the 1920s. W. C. Handy had given birth to the blues just a few blocks away and people like Ma Rainey and Bessie Smith were spreading the music around the world. But this is Harold's story, of how he refused to give up a dream, a dream that compelled him to work his way off the streets and into that golden circle of those who were invited to play the Palace Theatre.

Here is the sight, the sounds and the smell of Beale Street, the street of dreams, the street of magic, as Harold first sees it, from its heyday and on into the 1950s when Elvis took the music and gave it to the world...and when there was nothing left of Beale Street but some ghosts playing their blues in the night...

HOLLOWAY HOUSE PUBLISHING CO.
8060 Melrose Ave., Los Angeles, California 90046

Gentlemen I enclose $ _____ ☐ cash ☐ check ☐ money order, payment in full for books ordered. I understand that if I am not completely satisfied. I may return my order within 10 days for a complete refund. (Add 90¢ per order to cover postage and handling. California residents add 25¢ sales tax. Please allow three weeks for delivery.)

☐ **BH356-4 MEMPHIS BLUES $3.50**

Name _____

Address _____

City _____ State _____ Zip _____